TH
DESC
OF THE LYRE

Will Buckingham

ROMAN *Books*
www.roman-books.co.uk

Copyright © 2012 Will Buckingham

ISBN 978-93-80905-85-3

Typeset in Adobe Garamond Pro

First published 2012
This edition published 2014

1 3 5 7 9 8 6 4 2

British Library Cataloguing in Publication Data.
A catalogue record for this book is available from the British Library.

Publisher: Suman Chakraborty

ROMAN Books
26 York Street, London W1U 6PZ, United Kingdom
Unit 49, Park Plaza, South Block, Ground Floor, 71, Park Street, Kolkata 700016, WB, India
2nd Floor, 38/3, Andul Road, Howrah 711109, WB, India
www.roman-books.co.uk | www.romanbooks.co.in

Printed and bound in India by
Repro India Ltd

For Peter

For Orpheus' lute was strung with poets' sinews,
Whose golden touch could soften steel and stones...

The Two Gentlemen of Verona
William Shakespeare

The Chapel

The pilgrim path from the village of Trigrad is unmarked, so narrow that it is impossible to walk two abreast. You spend an hour asking around before you are pointed to the track that begins behind the small hotel, and that climbs up the hill to plunge into the dark pine forest where the air is still and windless. You emerge above the trees a half mile further up, where the path winds upwards in broad, snakelike curves. As you climb, the track becomes rockier and steeper. Lizards scuttle away at the sound of approaching footsteps. In the trees, birds call warning cries to each other. The grass hums with the electricity of insect life.

There are tortoises to be found here, if you are lucky or patient enough. They lumber through the undergrowth on the lower slopes, going about their prehistoric business. Once, in another age, the infant Hermes took one and hollowed it, stretching cowgut over the echoing shell: kithara, guitarra, guitar. But where you are going is further up, past the brow of the hill and across the broad meadow filled with flowers. Here, if you look up, you can see hawks circling, watching you from above with an unimaginable clarity. As you cross the meadow, you pick a single flower: it is yellow, with five petals. You climb the fence at the far end of the meadow, and take another track that curves through a copse of oak trees. Beyond the copse is a walled compound. The whitewash is faded grey, the painting on the roundel above the entrance arch so weathered that it is impossible to make it out whether it is an angel, a guardian or a saint.

Inside the compound, a spring burbles to itself, the fresh water flowing into a basin green with moss, then draining away along a little channel, out of the compound and down the hill.

Behind the spring is a half-ruined chapel, the walls covered with ivy. You bend to drink the water. It is fresh and cool.

The chapel door is unlocked. Inside, it takes a few seconds for your eyes to adjust to the light. The walls and ceiling are daubed with clumsy frescoes: high overhead, Christ Pantocrator looks down with his fingers held up in a Boy Scout's salute of blessing. The four Evangelists clutch their books as if their lives depended on it. But it is the image on the far wall, at the eastern end, that takes your attention. He is a saint, his body massive and his expression solemn. His beard is dark, and the corners of his mouth are turned down. He wears a brown robe. Over his shoulder is slung a red cape, joined with a clasp at the neck. His eyes are turned a little towards the heavens, but they seem nevertheless to draw your gaze. Around the saint's head is a halo of flaking gold. His hands are raised to either side of his body in an ancient gesture of prayer. Wrapped around the palms and wrists are bandages, so that only the tops of the long, fine fingers protrude. In his lap is the figure-of-eight body of a guitar, the neck slanting upwards over his left shoulder. The inscription above the figure's head can barely be made out; but if you trace the Cyrillic letters, you can see three words: Ivan Gelski, Svetets. Ivan Gelski, saint.

Yet the lives of the saints, the hagiographies and concordances, the encyclopaedias and church documents, say nothing of Ivan Gelski. Were it not for this chapel wall, here in the hills of the Rhodope mountains, were it not for the stories and the rumours that persist even now—the tales of a bandit called Ivan who became skilled in the art of music, who met his martyrdom at the age of thirty-three in Paris, who returned home a living saint—then it might seem as if he had never existed at all.

Today, it seems, you are the only pilgrim. You feel the sweat from the climb cooling on your body. You lean forwards and, unbeliever that you are, take the flower you have picked in the meadow to lay gently on the ledge before the image. Then— because it seems the right thing to do, because there is nobody here to witness your act, because the saint is gazing at you now with undiminished gravity—you go down on your knees, you close your eyes, and you listen.

Part One

The Bridegroom

1

The music was already there before he was born. He lay in his mother's womb and listened to her heart thud like a tupan. His eyes were closed, but his ears attuned to the rhythms of his mother's body—the unsteady ruchenitsas of her laughter, the slowing and quickening kopanitsas of her changing moods, the steady pravo horo of the hours she spent weaving at the loom. The music was there, as if awaiting his arrival, lying in ambush for him as he made his way down the road that led into existence.

He was the first of his mother's children to live beyond the womb, the first to open his eyes and see the soft green of the upland fields and meadows of the village of Gela. An elder brother and sister, twins, had died the year before his birth. His mother would later consider him to be not the first, but the third.

The music was already there, not only before his birth, but before his conception. His uncle, his mother's brother, had been a musician. His name, also, was Ivan. And he plucked the strings of the tambura with such sweetness it was said to bring peace to the animals of the forest, to calm the hearts of bears and wolves, so that they would lumber away and cause nobody any harm. Like Orfei, the old women of the village said: like Orfei, who once had been king. But uncle Ivan had killed himself in the spring before the child's birth, whilst his nephew swam, no larger than the length of a human thumb, in the many rhythms of his mother's womb.

They found the body hanging from a cherry tree, drenched in a rain of yellow blossom. When the fruits budded and swelled later that year, they were more abundant than anybody could remember.

Nobody asked why uncle Ivan took his life. In times such as these—when the countryside was full of robber bands who would cut a man's throat for a few coins, when Sultan Selim III sat uneasily on his throne listening to a million insects gnawing at the foundations of the empire, when those who toiled for a living on the hillsides were at the mercy of the rich, as they always are and always have been—in times such as these, what requires explanation is not why a man should wish to die, but rather why life persists at all.

A child, no more than seven or eight, brought the news of the suicide. Wandering on the hillside he had seen the man's body hanging from the tree. He ran to the village in tears. The dead man's sister, on hearing the news, touched her hand to her belly, retired to the house and closed the door. Through her tears she murmured blessings upon the child; and the child, shut in the singing, pulsing cauldron of her womb, listened as she sang her brother's name, over and over, two syllables, the second stressed, like the uneven steps of a dance: Ivàn, Ivàn, Ivàn.

2

The woman gave birth when the crops were ready for harvesting. She lay upon a bed of straw in the half-darkness of the cellar, moaning in pain. Around her bustled the midwife, an old baba who had climbed the track that led from Shiroka Luka, a sickle, a clutch of herbs and a bottle of plum brandy in her bag. The midwife upturned the open pots, so the birth might be a good one. Then the mother of the woman's husband built a fire. The midwife warmed water, preparing a bath with iron nails, that the baby might be strong and fearless, then she doused the blade of the sickle in brandy and passed it through the flames.

The birth was as easy as a birth can be, but the child was slippery and fell through the old baba's hands into the rough straw. It was then that the baby let out its first cry, a cry of anger with nothing melodious about it. The mother-in-law inclined her head. 'Such omens,' she said, smoothing the sweat-drenched hair from her daughter-in-law's brow. 'Such omens!' And she thought to herself: one day this child will take to the hillsides with the haiduti. It was a thought in which terror and pride were equally weighted.

The baba retrieved the baby and cut the umbilical cord with the sickle. She took the child and washed it in the warm water, then she salted the child's skin and wrapped it in a shirt belonging to the father. Only then did she hand the child to its mother who held the small voyager to her breast, feeling the pulse of the fragile life that had so recently been separated from her.

That evening, the father took the placenta, wrapped in an embroidered bag, to the foot of the cherry tree. The sun was sinking behind the hills and the air perfumed with the smell of late summer. The following day would be the day of the Holy Cross. Back in the village, the women were weaving their baskets and the men sharpening their knives for the coming festival.

The father dug the dry soil at the foot of the tree. When he had gone three feet down, he lowered the bag into the earth and shovelled the earth back on top. The valley was almost in shadow now and the air cool. The father put down his spade and smiled, one of those rare moments of happiness in which it seems that a single passing moment is sufficient to outweigh the entire weight of the world's sorrows. He reached up, took a single cherry and placed it in his mouth. Then, his shovel over his shoulder, he returned to the village.

3

The child's mother did not speak the name that was in her heart; but when she was alone with the infant, in the forty days of her confinement, she murmured it again and again: Ivàn, Ivàn, Ivàn. This was the child's name, and she knew it could not be otherwise.

When the godfather at last came to name the child and bring its first set of clothes, it was as she had guessed. He arrived at the house, drank the health of the family and the child, and spoke the name: the child is to be called Ivan, he said, as his uncle was also Ivan.

The name was inauspicious: it spoke of blossom, and music and death. Yet the child lived. He lived through the early months and through the first winter, and by the following spring he was gurgling with delight at the yellow and purple flowers in the upland meadows. When he took his first steps, his mother made a loaf drenched in honey and passed out chunks of warm, sweet bread to her neighbours, so that he might grow to be strong and quick.

It did not seem long before the child held an axe in his hand for the first time, before he went to cut wood in the forest, before he learned how to draw milk from a goat and how to slaughter a sheep. And all this time, the armed bands went to and fro across the hillsides, travellers came and went on their long and dusty paths, merchants buying and selling, officials going about the business of empire, demanding food and drink, lodgings for the night, and taxes the following morning to compensate for the wear to their teeth. All this time the fates spun that dark cloth in which only a few threads of silver or gold could be discerned, but the child went on living, bearing his name with him, his name that spoke of blossom, music and death.

4

For a traveller walking along the mountain roads after dark, the presence of the village is all but invisible. For even though tonight is the night before the wedding is due to take place, the village lies in darkness. Not a single light gleams from the houses that cluster to the hillside like rocks and stones; and were it not for the dogs who bark at their own echoes across the valley—when will they ever learn?—and for the little smoke that rises from the chimneys to obscure the stars, it would be possible to walk within a few yards of the settlement and to remain quite unaware of its presence. Such is the lawlessness of the land that cheerful illuminations and lamps to light the traveller's way would draw thieves and scoundrels as surely as they would draw fluttering armies of night insects. It is not a time for celebration. The year is 1811, and between the heavy taxation by officials, and the lawlessness that has spread like a black plague through the mountains, there is little cause for joy. But even in the darkest of times, life must go on: there must be births, weddings, funerals; crops must be planted, tended and harvested. Life persists, if only because it does not know what else to do.

Seventeen years have passed since the musician Ivan hanged himself from a cherry tree. He is long dead, buried with his tambura by his side. Few can remember the sweetness of his music. And the child who bears his name (the same child who, only a moment ago it seems—how quickly time passes—was born in a dark cellar) is now of a marriageable age. He is grown taller than both his mother and his father, and broad too, so that, although young, he fills any room that he enters with his presence. His moustache is dark, and gives him a handsome, serious air. He is an unusually silent boy, inclined neither to laughter nor to merriment. He does not read or write. The hillsides and the forests have been the sole places of his schooling; but he can read these hillsides and forests as well as any scholar can his books.

The girl who is to be his bride is a year his junior. She is beautiful and as skilled in the work of the hand—with the loom and the needle—as she is in weaving sweet tunes with her voice. Several months ago Ivan took her posy at the sedyanka, whilst the girls sewed and sang and told stories, sitting knee to knee with the village boys. She lowered her eyes, but did not ask for the flowers back. Ivan placed the posy in his hat, so all could see that the girl consented. It is perhaps strange that the stories that have come down to us do not furnish the girl with a name; and so to compensate for this negligence, it is necessary to act as godfather, to name her where history is silent. Let her name be Stoyanka: she who is steadfast.

Ivan and Stoyanka prepare for their wedding in separate houses. The groom's mother has placed apples upon the grave of her brother and has sung melodies to the earth where he lies, songs that are part lament and part invitation, for death should not bar a man from attending a wedding. She has offered wine to saint Georgi, on his white horse, and saint Dimitar, on his red horse. She has placed another glass of wine before the Mother of God, and invited her without expectation of her attendance. The Mother of God, after all, is frequently preoccupied with matters of high importance. She cannot be expected to attend to every wedding in every mountain village in every quarter of the world; yet there is a chance that, at the very least, she might send a blessing, or a low-ranking angel, or a portion of grace.

Finally, the mother has poured wine on the roots of the local trees—the cherry tree in the branches of which her brother met his end, the apple tree behind the house, the circular grove of ancient oaks that Orfei had caused, through the playing of his lyre, to dance the horo—so that the trees too might incline their branches towards the feast. The wedding bread has been prepared, poured with honey. The poles have been cut for the wedding banners. And now that everything is in order, the village sleeps. The sad songs of parting have been sung in the house of the bride; the dancing in the house of the groom is over, and the guests have retired to their beds. It is early on Sunday morning, and not even the dogs are barking.

The horsemen make their way silently through the trees. There are thirty-one of them in all, armed with guns and with swords sheathed in their belts. Their faces are lit only by the faint light of a half moon. They wear turbans upon their heads, and on their faces are expressions of twitching vigilance. At their head is a rider so large that his horse sways uncomfortably and, every so often, stumbles beneath him, sending stones skittering down the slopes of the mountain. He sweats a little. The moonlight and sheen of sweat make him look as feverish as a ghost from the marshes.

The horses emerge from the fringes of the forest, and look down on the silent village. The large man squints into the darkness, but can see nothing. Then he notices a ribbon of smoke that blots out the stars. There, in the heart of the village, the girl is sleeping. He turns to the troops. 'Three of you,' he says, 'remain with me on the ridge. The rest of you, head down to the village. Bring her back to me.'

They mount the ridge of the hill, the dark forest behind them. The village waits, as if it knows what is coming. Then the raiding party, twenty-seven well-armed men, spur their horses and clatter down the hill, sending small avalanches of stone and mud before them. The fat man—he is the son of the Pasha, and has seen the girl many times, going to and from the well—adjusts his weight in the saddle.

Lights appear in the village, then shouts. Men are rising from their beds, snatching guns from beside their pillows. Women are taking up pokers, kitchen knives, and scythes should they need to defend their virtue. Dogs—waking from dreams in which they finally meet those rivals from across the valley who always bark last—leap to their feet and draw back their lips, snarling and yelping. The twenty-seven horses are close to the village now. The Pasha's son waits on the ridge with his guard, immobile, pale and silent. There is a shudder of gunfire, shots loosed into the air, as the horses gallop across the bridge over the stream and into the village. Then there is silence. The horses have stopped in the village square. A man dismounts. He walks slowly to the door of a house close to the village centre and there, outside the door, he waits. From inside, he can hear the voices of women.

'I wish to harm nobody,' he calls. 'We have come only for the bride.'

No sound comes from inside. His words are swallowed by the hot darkness of the night. The dogs cringe in the shadows. The men wait behind their bolted doors, their guns loaded. The horsemen are Turks, they murmur to each other. They lower their guns, for it is a crime to kill a Turk. Tonight there will be no slave revolt, no glorious revolution, no rising up of the oppressed. There will be only the hope that they may be spared the worst, and the fear that they will only be spared for more terrible things to come.

The man takes his rifle and hammers upon the closed door with the butt. 'Bring out the girl who is to be married tomorrow,' he shouts. 'I come for the bride.'

Again there is silence. Then the door opens and a woman—

a woman no longer young, perhaps, but still beautiful and upright—comes into the street. 'Please,' she says, 'not the girl. Take me if you must, but not my daughter.'

'We have come for the girl,' the man outside repeats. 'The girl who was to be wed tomorrow. Are you the mother?'

The woman steps forward and rocks her head in assent. She kneels down on the floor and reaches out, as if to embrace the waist of the man who stands over her. The scene is almost one of silence, shot through only with the sobs and mutterings of the women inside, and the purr of night insects. The man steps back, so that the woman grasps hold of only empty space. 'Do not take her,' the woman says. 'I will go with you, but not my daughter.'

The man lifts his rifle and swings the butt at the woman's cheek. She crumples to one side. The blood is invisible in the darkness and shadow, but when she raises her hand to her cheek it comes away wet. The man faces the dark doorway of the house. 'Bring out the girl!' he calls. 'We are many and we are armed.'

In the doorway, a pale apparition. Stoyanka, decked out in her white bridal costume, trimmed with red, her hair braided and woven with flowers, steps through the darkness. She looks at the man before her. She does not look down at her mother, who lies in the dirt, sobbing. Instead she stands before the man who has come for her and looks at him with such fierce directness that he almost takes a step back.

'You come for a bride with guns,' she says, 'but what use is a bride with a bullet in her heart?'

The man does not reply. He simply waits.

'Tell me,' Stoyanka says, 'who is the man who has business with me?'

'He is your husband,' the man smiles. 'You are to be married.'

'And where does he wait?'

27

'Upon the hill. He is mounted on a horse and dressed in green brocade.'

The girl does not flinch. 'My betrothed has no horse. He does not wait upon the hill, but instead in the house of his mother and father. He may not wear green, but dresses in red and white.'

The man smiles. 'But your betrothed is poor, and the man to whom I shall bring you is rich. Your betrothed does not read or write, yet the man who you will marry has the knowledge of many books. Your betrothed is in bondage, but the man to whom I shall bring you will honour you in marriage and make you free.'

'And love?' the girl asks. Her mother lets out a sob from where she lies on the ground. 'What about love?'

'He has love enough,' says the man. 'And if you also have love, you will accompany me.'

The girl hesitates. 'And if I do not?'

'Then we will take your mother and we will kill her. We will seize your father and cut his throat. The worst, however, we will reserve for your betrothed, whom we will impale upon a stake at dawn, so his cries may still be heard long into the following night. And so I say again: if you also have love, you will accompany me.'

The girl takes off her bridal headdress and bends down. She hands the headdress to her mother. 'Keep this for me,' she whispers. 'I must go.' Then she stands again. 'The man who waits for me,' she says with a coldness that seems for a moment to chill the humid summer air, 'can do what he wills, but I will not love him. I will go with him, I will be his companion, I will do all he asks, but in our union there will be neither love nor the fruits of love. For I love only one, and nothing can turn my heart.'

Then, without saying goodbye to her mother or to her father

who stands in the shadows with his pistol, she follows the man back to his horse and mounts behind him. 'Up on the ridge,' the man says, pointing to the dark smudge of trees, 'your husband is waiting.'

The party starts to move off, a clatter of hooves. As they come to the bridge, which only three horses can cross abreast, they see a dark figure blocking the road on the far side. The man at their head holds up a hand. In the faint moonlight he sees the face of a young man, a boy. The boy is unarmed and dressed as a groom before a wedding.

'Stoyanka,' the boy says, looking directly at the girl who is mounted behind the leader of the band.

The horses come to a halt only five or six yards away. 'Move, boy,' says the horseman. He draws his weapon from his belt.

'Stoyanka,' the boy says again. His speaks the name as if it were a spell or a talisman that might guard him from danger.

The horseman lifts his gun. The two men to either side do so as well.

'Stoyanka,' he says a third time.

The horseman takes aim. At the moment he is about to fire, the girl behind him throws her weight to one side, unbalancing him. The gun goes off, a single shot. The boy who was standing in the road crumples to the ground, holding his leg and crying out in agony. The horseman regains his balance and spurs the horse onwards, the girl still behind him. The boy smells the sweat of twenty-seven horses galloping past, and waits for another bullet. A deafening rage floods his ears, louder than the roar of the one hundred and eight hooves pounding upon the cobblestones of the bridge.

The second bullet does not come, and the sound of the horses subsides; but the rage continues to blot out everything else. The boy lies in the damp night grass in his wedding costume, blood running from his thigh, and in his ears thuds the discordant fury of pain.

Beneath the bridge, the clear mountain stream runs down towards the plains, as it has done ever since the time of Orfei.

5

The Pasha's son waited, watching his men flood across the bridge and back towards the hill. The single gunshot had caused him to sweat. The horse beneath him sighed a little. The village was now in uproar. Shutters were thrown open, torches lit, men running into the streets, women wailing, tearing their hair, babies crying, dogs barking, even chickens, woken from their roosts, letting out squawks and cries. It was almost soothing to watch the bewilderment and the pain from such a distance, the scurrying figures with torches, the moans of anger and distress.

When the horses were clear of the village and climbing the hill, they slowed to a walk. The men remained vigilant. They had left the settlement with barely a challenge, other than the foolish boy who had tried to block their path; but then they had not expected to be challenged. The villagers knew that, were they to resist, they would court even greater sufferings. Nevertheless, the men on horseback were wary. They would not be happy until they were clear of the village and the farmland that surrounded it. The people in those parts were rough and unpredictable. There was no telling what fool might chance cocking his gun at the retreating party.

The Pasha's son watched the line of horses as it wound up the hill. In the moonlight, he could see the bride, his bride, her clothing pale. He smiled to himself, and ran his tongue over his lips, tasting the sweat and the cool scent of the night.

6

When the villagers found the boy by the bridge, he was already unconscious, lying with his head lolling down the bank. They held up torches to see and then, having cut through the fabric of his wedding suit, washed the wound in the clear water from the stream. The boy breathed erratically as they carried him back to his village where his mother was waiting.

His mother—the same woman who, many years before, had suffered the death of a brother in a blizzard of yellow cherry blossom, who had given birth to a child on the damp straw of a cellar, attended by a midwife with a bag full of charms, but older now, her jet-black hair turning to grey—took him into her house and there she embraced his unconscious body. She laid him on his bed and prepared herbs to clean and wash the wound. Meanwhile, from the house of the abducted bride came the sound of keening and mourning: they had expected to lose a daughter that evening; but not in this fashion, not to a man such as this.

The boy's mother paid no attention to their grief. She boiled water and steeped it with the herbs she had picked on the hillsides and had hung to dry by the fire, then she washed the boy's wound. At the first touch of the stinging liquid, the boy let out a small cry. The mother took this to be a good sign. The bullet was still lodged in the flesh. She pressed at his thigh, hoping it might come out easily, but it remained fast. She called her husband and, whilst she held her son, he took a knife from the kitchen and prised the bullet free. When they had finished, they sat until dawn, watching over him. Her lips moved with his name: Ivàn, Ivàn, Ivàn.

Not long after, the summer started to turn to autumn and a chill came into the air. The festival of Golyama Bogoroditsa, the feast of the mother of God, came round; and the boy's father— because his son's wound was still livid and the boy burned with a fever—set out across the mountains to make offerings at the monastery of Bachkovo. He took with him a cheese in a cloth and some bread, and walked for three days, sleeping where he could, drinking from the forest streams. He had no horse or cart to carry him, and he went on foot away from the major paths, crossing upland meadows that were blooming with flowers. He feasted without joy on the black berries that hung from the brambles. At night he lit small fires to keep away the wolves and the bears. And at last he arrived at the monastery, emerging from the mountains onto the road that led up to the shrine.

The feast day was the following morning, and the road was crowded with pilgrims. Traders were selling griddled fish and bread, bundles of medicinal herbs, charms and forged relics. On that particular morning, one could have bought as many as seventeen thumbs of Saint John the Baptist. Ivan's father had only a few coins in his pockets, and the crowds made him uneasy. Somewhere, a little way off, he could hear the bleating tones of a gaida, the bagpipe that wailed like a lost sheep on a hillside, crying for its mother. Ivan's father lowered his eyes and pushed through the crowds, following them up the hill until he came to the threshold of the monastery. He bowed his head and entered the courtyard.

Inside it was less a peaceful sanctuary than a rowdy marketplace, monks and dogs scratching themselves in the sun and in the sight of God, hawkers selling candles and phials and icons. A long line of pilgrims stood, waiting to be admitted to the church. Not knowing what else to do, he asked the last in line, 'Tell me, where might I find the Virgin?'

The man smiled amicably. 'She waits inside,' he said. 'You must simply join the line. Tell me, have you come far?'

Ivan's father mumbled the name of his village, but the other man had not heard of it. Many of the pilgrims were well-dressed, and for a moment Ivan's father felt ashamed of his clothes; but he reminded himself that God is interested neither in the fabrics with which the body is clothed nor in the flesh with which the soul is clothed, but He cares only for the soul itself, whatever that might be, wherever it might be found.

Ivan's father had been to the shrine once before, when he himself was a boy. Now it was grander than he remembered, and richer. The monks wore clothes more opulent than before. When he had visited as a boy, he had run through the courtyard shouting, sending chickens flapping off in squawking flurries. This time, things were different. His hair was grey. There was no joy in him. He kept his head down, not pausing to gawp at the people and paintings. His thoughts were only of his son.

The line shuffled forwards, and before long, Ivan's father had stepped out of the sun and into the narthex. He could hear the intoning of liturgies from inside the nave, could smell the thick scent of the incense. I know nothing of religion, he told himself. I am unlearned in books and scriptures. I do not know the ways of God, nor would I recognise Him if I met Him upon the hillside.

As he entered the church, the smell of the incense became stronger, catching at the back of his throat. Why must God smell like this? he found himself thinking. Why can He not have a good, clean smell, like the smell of fresh cheese, or of the meadows in summer? Why this thick, sweet darkness? Then he looked up and gasped, because the interior of the church was both wonderful and terrible. The liturgy murmured around him in call and response, the priest behind the iconostasis took the lead and hidden voices replied. The icons glowed in the light of a hundred candles. And although he could not read the words, the pictures spoke to him. He saw Saint John, that fierce and unruly angel of the desert, his body covered with a thick pelt of hair like an animal, broad wings stretching from his back; he saw Dimitar and Georgi on their horses, Dimitar about to deal the death blow to a human adversary, Georgi about to dispatch a dragon (but why? he asked himself. He could not remember). He saw the Virgin and the Christ-child, and was reassured that the Mother of God would surely help him, for she had lost her son, as he feared he might lose his, and if there was any saint who would understand the anguish of such loss, it would be the Virgin.

Then he was standing before her, the Virgin Mary Eleusa, her features in shadow, only the silverwork glinting in the flickering light of the candles. Three steps led up to her, and the man in front of him was leaning his forehead against her, making an offering. Ivan's father waited for him to descend, and then he himself climbed the steps. Only a foot away from the Virgin, he could still not make out her features. He touched the silverwork, peering into the shadows to see if he could see the lips of the icon move, then he reached into his pocket and laid a coin in front of her. He looked the Virgin in the eye, for it is a weak man who cannot look a woman in the eye, and he spoke to her, under his breath. I give you my son, he said. If you only cure him of his sickness and his fever, I give him to your keeping. And may you and the holy saints do with him what you will.

Mary did not respond, but nor did she look away. Behind him, the people standing in line were becoming restless. Somebody muttered he should move on. There were people

35

waiting. Ivan's father lowered his gaze. He turned away from the Virgin, and saw the light piercing the dome of the church in great shafts that swirled with the smoke of incense, and there were tears in his eyes. The drone of the liturgy and the exhaustion of his three-day trek to the monastery, the crowds who were pressing on all sides, the incense-sweetness that was the smell of God, too sweet for him, a rough man of the mountains—all these pressed upon him with such force that he swayed on the steps as he descended, and were it not for the kindness of the other pilgrims, he would have collapsed altogether.

Those kind people led him back into the sunlight, and sat him down to catch his breath. There were tears on his cheeks, which he wiped with his sleeve. Beyond the murmur of the liturgy, he could hear the mournful bleat of the gaida, a long way off. And then, because everything he had come to do he had done, he rose to his feet and left the monastery, fleeing the crowds and market-traders and revellers and pilgrims as he headed up the path back into the mountains.

He did not stop until he was sure he was alone, and there he drank cold water and ate fresh blackberries. He looked in his pouch. There was still a little bread, and cheese enough to sustain him. Perhaps, he thought, when I return home, the Virgin will have had a chance to act. But he was worried all the same. There were so many petitioners. The Virgin could no more be expected to respond to every prayer than she could be expected to attend every wedding. With this melancholy thought, he started on his way back home.

7

Whether—after his father's long pilgrimage—the Virgin intervened or not is unclear. By the time Ivan's father returned from the monastery, dog-tired and sore-footed, the boy was sitting up in bed and taking soup from a ladle, sometimes even a little bread; but his skin was still hot to the touch and his forehead continued to burn. His wound was healing a little, and the inflammation had gone down, but the fever persisted, and with it the discordant fury that raged in his ears, and that did not let up for a single moment.

The autumn turned to winter, thick snow covered the hillside, and even though his mother pressed cold snow in fistfuls to his forehead, the fever's rage went unstilled. Where before he had been beardless, now his beard grew. Where in the past he had been well-fed and handsome, now his cheeks became hollowed out and his eyes sunk into their sockets. Across his skin crawled a red rash from the heat and the sweat and the hours spent unmoving in his bed, and it itched terribly, so that he tore at it with his nails until the blood flowed, scratched at himself as if this blood-letting might allow the rage to escape; but this only made things worse, his raw flesh rubbing up against the rough, waxy sheepskins where he lay for the whole of the winter.

If this was sickness and fever, it was not a fever of the body so much as of the soul. For if all of the saints, from the most lowly up to the Mother of God, care for our bodies, it has always been the case that we are responsible, in the end, for our souls. The source of the heat was not a poison in his blood nor the shock of the bullet that had torn through his now healed flesh, but instead it was a blinding, white-hot rage that had taken root in him on that evening on the bridge, when Stoyanka was taken from him. Sometimes, in the night, he howled so loud that he set the dogs of the village barking, and he only fell into a fitful sleep at dawn. Sometimes he simply lay repeating the name of his beloved over and over again: Stoyanka, Stoyanka, Stoyanka.

The cold months passed slowly, the cycle of festival and feast and fasting: from Andreevden when they throw boiled grain up the chimney to calm the hunger of the bears, to Varvara when the needles and knives are hidden for fear of smallpox; from Varvara to Sava, Nikulden, Ignazhden and Koleda, on which there was no singing at the door of Ivan's house, and from Koleda to the Dirty Days that follow when the sky and the earth remain unchristened and evil spirits walk the land; and then to Ivanovden, dedicated to the Baptist who lives wild in the desert with his strange, angelic wings, and Babinden the day of midwives, and Trifonovden for the pruning of the vines, and Haralampi for the keeping away of plague, and the days of spring cleaning when household things are swept and dusted and folded and put in their proper places; until the first of March, when the limping Baba rises up from her bed, her spine twisted and temper ill-disposed, and ushers in the coming warmth.

It was only then, on Baba Marta when the people were exchanging martenitsas fashioned of red and white twisted threads, that Ivan pushed back the blankets and rose from his sick bed, declaring the fever had passed. His mother put her hand to his forehead and saw that it was so, and held him in her arms and cried; but his father saw that the fever still burned, a black light in the young man's eyes, a hard cast to his mouth.

Ivan asked for bread, and he breakfasted more heartily than he had done since Stoyanka was taken. He left the house and went down to the stream where he stripped naked and washed his suffering body. Then he returned home and asked his father to give him his gun and his mother to provide him with food. Having eaten, he told his mother to bring him his wedding costume. His mother brought it to him. The white woollen trousers were stitched together where the bullet had torn through. Very slowly, the young man dressed as for a wedding. When he was done, he set his wedding headdress upon his head, and said, 'I am going to the mountains, for I cannot bear to remain here. What wife can I take when the one I was to wed has been taken from me? What joy can there be for me in this house?'

His mother recalled the moment of his birth, when he had slipped from the midwife's hands and fallen to the floor, and knowing that fate's cloth is woven in ways too subtle to understand, the threads bound so very tight, she said nothing. Instead, she embraced him.

'But what will you find in the mountains?' his father asked, looking into his son's face for any trace of softness, finding none.

'I go to the mountains to find peace,' he said.

'And how will you find peace?' asked his father.

Ivan looked down. 'I will find peace through the blood of those who have caused me pain,' he said. Then he turned and left the house, dressed as if for a wedding, a rifle upon his back, heading across the hillsides where Orfei once walked; and his father watched him go, until he was lost in the trees.

8

Bogdan Voyvoda sat at the mouth of the cave and contemplated old age. He was approaching forty, and his hair was already grey. His teeth on the left side had almost entirely gone—several knocked out in a fight when he was still a boy, and the remainder pulled out ten years before on account of the decay that otherwise would have killed him. It had been an agonising operation, despite the fierce rakiya he had consumed to dull the pain. Lacking the tools of a surgeon, the procedure had been carried out with hot tongs there on the hillside, his men pinning him down by the arms and the legs, two holding his jaws open, and one seated upon his chest, his standard-bearer being the one who held the tongs. Even now, as he sat looking over the hillside, his tongue pushed into the corners of his mouth and, without it being exactly conscious, a memory of the pain of that morning shuddered through him.

Bogdan was born of those mountains, and wanted nothing more than to die there, at peace, and to be buried in the soil that had nourished him. He was a short man. When he stood, his feet planted on the ground, he seemed broader and more massive than he actually was. He didn't smile often.

He was dressed in a white tunic and trousers. Around his shoulders was a woollen blanket, and he wore a woollen hat to keep his brains warm. It helped him think. Cold brains, he believed, were the root cause of much of the world's stupidity. His men had now returned from the places where they had spent the winter in hiding. Every year, when the snows began to melt, they joined him in the grove where the trees stood in a circle; and they spent the short months of late spring and summer together, raiding and exacting revenge for wrongs both real and imagined, before departing to their separate places of refuge in the cold months. If in the winter the hills are filled with shepherds with their flocks, in the summer they are the preserve of haiduti. Behind every pear tree a rifle may be cocked; behind every hill, a standard lifted to the skies; in each beech wood, a rebel waiting.

Bogdan did not return to his home village in the winter months. Instead he walked west until he came to the small monastery not far from Skopje. There he was welcomed as a brother, and he spent the winter dressed in the robes of a priest, under the protection of God. It was not out of piety that he took refuge there, but out of need; and if he prayed to God at night in his cell throughout the winter, he did so without any conviction that his prayers were being heard. He was not a man made for things of the spirit. He loved only those things that he could hold in his hands, the dark earth, the sparkling water that he lifted to his lips in his cupped palms.

He had taken to the hills as a young man, after witnessing the death of his father. His father had been a thief, having been of a constitution unsuited to the labour of the plough. He had stolen so that his family might flourish, and they did indeed flourish, because a thief will often prosper where an honest man will fail. But he was caught one day making off with a golden drinking-cup belonging to an Ottoman official, and was thrown immediately into prison. A protracted trial was not necessary, for the theft had been plain, and it is a serious thing to take a golden cup from an official. The thief was taken into the marketplace, tied to the ground between four stakes, arms and legs splayed. The villagers were driven out of their houses so they might witness the killing. Then a stake was sharpened with a knife, and driven from the bottom to the top of his spine. The executioners were skilled. When the stake emerged by the neck, the spine remained unbroken. The thief's legs were fastened to the stake and he was lifted upright. It took him two days to die, two days during which the site of execution was guarded so no villager might come in the night with a knife and put the wrong-doer out of his misery. After these two days of hearing his father's moans Bogdan had fled to the hills. He had been there ever since, for twenty-five years.

Bogdan Voyvoda had repaid the barbarism meted out to his father in the same coin, and many times over, and in doing so he had created a name for himself. When convoys passed through that part of the mountains, they quivered with fear at the name of Bogdan Voyvoda. Many stories were told about him. In some Bogdan was short, in others he was tall. There were those who said that he had a hump upon his back or that he walked with a limp, and others who said that he was the most handsome of men. In truth, few knew anything about him, other than his comrades, and the brothers with whom he spent his winter retreat. And Bogdan, although capable of cruelty, did not have the genius for brutality that affects some men, his revenge always tempered by the memory of the quiver that went through him as he saw his father tied to the four stakes as the fifth was slowly sharpened.

Still a boy, shortly after joining the haiduti who were then under the tutelage of another Voyvod, he had killed three men with a knife whilst they were sleeping. They were Turks, travelling along those mountain roads, and were no more guilty of his father's death than he was himself. The killing was carried out with the efficiency of a child of the mountains who had put many sheep to the slaughter; and the morning after, as he washed his knife in the stream and watched the blood flow away and the water run clear, he realised that he could never return home. He was wedded, from that moment on, to the mountains. And every spring, when he folded his robe and left the monastery, he did so with reluctance. If only I could stay, he would say to himself. But already his legs would be carrying him away from the monastery door.

Bogdan looked out of the cave mouth and saw a tall young man approaching along the path, dressed in his wedding clothes. He rolled his shoulders and leaned down to press his thumb into the earth—a gesture he often performed, unconsciously, for the sake of reassurance. He could have slipped back into the cave, for the young man was walking with his head down, and surely had not seen him. Instead, however, he simply watched, to see what would happen. The young man hesitated at a junction in the track and then turned left onto the path that wound below the mouth of Bogdan Voyvoda's cave. The brigand unhitched his knife, because it is always wise to have a knife to hand, and waited, his tongue probing the empty space where once there had been teeth. A lizard scuttled across the path, hesitated to sniff the air, and was gone into the undergrowth. The mouth of the cave was ten feet, no more than that, above the path. Bogdan continued to sit, looking down, his body motionless. It is remarkable, he often thought, how invisible he had become as a result of his friendship with the mountains. He was capable of standing no more than three feet away from his adversaries, and they would see nothing but the mountains, the trees and the meadows.

But when he approached, the boy looked up and saw the brigand immediately. Bogdan lifted up his right hand—he used his left for his knife—in a laconic greeting. The boy took off his headdress.

Ivan had been walking for two days, first west over the hills from Gela, and then south towards the Muglenska river. There he had spent a hungry night, waking before dawn and turning north, following the banks until he was just south of Teshel. From there he had taken a path southwards until he reached the gorge that led to Trigrad, where the river plunged into the ground through a hole that gaped wide amongst the rocks, at the place they called the Devil's Throat. It was here, they said, that Orfei entered the underworld in pursuit of his lost love. And it was along this mountain path that Ivan met with Bogdan Voyvoda.

'You are far from the wedding, it seems,' observed the brigand.

'My bride is gone,' Ivan said.

'And you seek her on this lonely path?'

'I seek another.'

Bogdan Voyvoda smiled. 'Another bride? You are fickle, young man.'

'I have only one bride,' Ivan said. 'But she is taken from me. What I seek is revenge.'

Bogdan Voyvoda chuckled. 'Revenge? Do you believe that revenge will be as sweet as the bride you have lost?'

Ivan thought about this. 'Revenge is always bitter,' he said.

Bogdan eased himself off the rock on which he was perched, and half slid down the hillside to the path. He took several steps forward to examine the boy, pausing right in front of him and looking straight into his eyes.

'Brides can also be bitter,' he said with a smile.

What happened next surprised them both. Ivan grasped hold of the brigand's tunic, and yanked him forwards, so that they were close enough to kiss. 'There was no bitterness in her,' he said. He gave the tunic a tug, as if he wanted to pull Bogdan Voyvoda to the ground. If this had indeed been his intention, he did not succeed. The brigand was strong, whilst the boy had spent the winter in high fever and was weak. In a moment, Ivan was on his back, and Bogdan was standing over him, one stocky leg to either side of Ivan's body, pointing the tip of his long knife at the boy's nose. 'Move,' said the brigand, 'and I will kill you.'

Ivan did not move.

'Now, tell me. This bride of yours. How do you suppose you will avenge her?'

There were tears in Ivan's eyes. 'I have come,' he said, 'for Bogdan Voyvoda. I wish to join with him.'

'But revenge is bitter. You will be adding bitterness to bitterness.'

'If I cannot have what is sweet,' Ivan said, 'then I will eat only what is bitter.'

'And what if you were to die, here on the mountains?' the brigand asked. 'I hear Bogdan Voyvoda is a cruel man, that he is without mercy.'

'Death, perhaps, will be less bitter than life,' Ivan said.

Bogdan Voyvoda drew the knife away and stepped to one side, so that he was no longer standing over the boy. Then he reached out a hand. 'Let me help you,' he said.

Ivan eyed him with suspicion.

'Let me help you.'

Ivan took the brigand's hand. The bandit helped the boy to his feet. Then he smiled. 'Welcome to the mountains,' he said. 'My name is Bogdan Voyvoda. If you want to come with me, then come. If you do not wish to do so, then as you are a stranger, and as I have no reason to trust you, I will free you from the bitterness of life, and let you take your chance on the next world. The choice is yours.'

'And if I do come with you?'

'Then there will be nothing for you but bitterness and more bitterness. We will sow seeds of bitterness in spring and reap the harvest as the summer comes to a close. Then in winter, we will rest. And if you betray me or my men, you will die.'

'Then I will come. I want nothing more than this.'

Bogdan Voyvoda looked pleased. 'Good,' he said. 'Tell me your name.'

'My name is Ivan.'

'And your village?'

'I come from the village of Gela.'

Bogdan Voyvoda smiled. 'And I am from Stoikite,' he said. 'So it seems that we are neighbours. Well, Ivan Gelski, I have white cheese and bread enough for two in the cave. There is coffee also. We will stay until sunset, and then we will leave.'

9

The cave narrowed a little way after the entrance, so that it was necessary to crawl. Ivan followed the haidut on all fours. The passageway turned a corner, opening out into a chamber that sang with the trickling of countless streams of water. In the middle of the chamber was a fire, ventilated by a flue that ran up into the darkness and sucked the smoke out to hover low over the hillside. Around the fire were several logs, to serve as sitting-places. Ivan followed Bogdan Voyvoda into the dark and settled down near the hearth. He watched as the haidut put the copper coffee pot over the flames. The dark, thick smell of coffee cut through the smoke. Not long after, Bogdan Voyvoda poured the coffee into a clay cup and passed it to Ivan. He handed him a piece of hard bread and some white cheese.

They ate in silence. The cave was cold, and the fire seemed to do little more than remind him of the fact. When they were finished eating, Bogdan Voyvoda threw handfuls of earth over the flames until they died down. He passed the young man a blanket to keep him warm. 'Tell me about her,' he said, his voice kindly. 'Was she beautiful?'

Ivan fingered the fringe of the blanket. Without the light from the fire, he could no longer see Bogdan Voyvoda's face. Whether his eyes were closed or open seemed to make little difference, so he closed them.

'She was beautiful,' he said.

'Her name,' said Bogdan Voyvoda. 'What was her name?'

'Stoyanka,' said Ivan. 'Her name was Stoyanka.' But he could say no more, because the mention of her name brought tears to his eyes. He put his head on his knees and started to sob.

The blow to the side of his face came so suddenly that he did not notice it until afterwards. Bogdan Voyvoda was crouching over him in the dark, one hand around his neck and the other raised for a second assault. Ivan struggled in the darkness. It seemed as if Bogdan Voyvoda had swelled to fill the entire cave, as if he had become the darkness of the cave, bearing down upon him. And, as if from a long way above, through the throbbing pain in his cheek Ivan heard Voyvoda's voice. 'Do not weep, Ivan. Take your tears and turn them to bitterness.'

Then Bogdan Voyvoda released the young man, who drew up his knees and hunched on the floor of the cave, closing his eyes to suppress the tears that were surging up through him like salt springs through the hard rocks of his misery. He bit together hard until his teeth hurt. Bogdan was right: tears were worthless. Ivan could smell tobacco smoke. When he opened his eyes, he saw a single red light where Bogdan Voyvoda was smoking a rough cigarette, made with papers torn from a book he had stolen. Ivan reached out his hand. 'Give me a smoke,' he said. Bogdan Voyvoda chuckled. 'Of course,' he said, and taking the cigarette from his own mouth he passed it to Ivan.

When Ivan had finished the cigarette, they sat in silence for a long while. Eventually Bogdan Voyvoda got to his feet. 'Stay here,' he said.

The bandit moved with absolute assurance through the dark towards the tunnel that led to the mouth of the cave. Ivan listened as the man crawled away into the dark, and then he was alone.

Sitting in the darkness, Ivan shivered. He could hear the thud of blood inside his skull, the rasp of his own breath; and the more he listened, the more the many sounds of his body seemed as if they were outside, as if they belonged more to the dark and echoing chamber of the cave, with its steady drip of cold water, than they did to him. He drew the blanket around himself more closely, but he no longer had a sense of where his body started and where it finished. He could have been as vast as a mountain or as small as a grain of sand, and it would have changed nothing. The only constant thing was the drip of water. And as he sat there, it was as if all his misery, all his suffering, was somehow transmuted into sound: the hot pain where his leg had been pierced by the bullet, the fury he did not know what to do with, that he clung to even as it burned him, the ache and discomfort of his body, suffering after such long illness, the memory of the time when he had imagined happiness, here in the world, might be possible. Ivan became the cave, or the cave became Ivan, or both were swallowed up in the endless echoing of discord and fury that rages at the very bottom of things; and all the time the water continued to drip: clear, pure drops falling through darkness, as they had done since before the world began. Ivan, or the cave, began to moan.

Bogdan returned at dusk, and as he crawled back into the cave, he could hear the strange, low moaning. He moved over to the boy and shook him gently. 'Come, Ivan,' he said. 'We must go. Follow me.' And Ivan reached out to Bogdan and touched the old bandit's face, and he was grateful.

Bogdan went ahead and Ivan followed. They crouched on all fours. When they came to the tunnel, they crawled until they could see the pale light of dusk. When they emerged into the night, Ivan was astonished at how warm the air was. The pains in his body seemed to awaken in the warmth, but there was something comforting about the unarguable clarity of physical pain. 'We have a long way to walk,' Bogdan Voyvoda said. 'You must follow, and you must keep silent.'

Bogdan Voyvoda went ahead, and Ivan followed. They moved

across the hillsides and through the forests, and as Ivan walked, the anger and rage continued to burn inside him, an echoing torrent of sound.

10

They traced a path along the gorge leading up to the caves at Trigrad. They stopped at the Devil's Throat, where the river fell roaring into the earth, and they rested a short while and drank water from the cool stream. Then they continued to where the cliffs opened out, and headed up over the hills to the west. Bogdan Voyvoda walked fast and did not glance back.

After a couple of hours, the clothes of both men were soaked through with sweat, but they continued at the same speed. Ivan, weakened from the long months he had spent in his sick bed, stumbled occasionally. He was hungry. But he said nothing. The moon rose over the pine trees, and a long way off a wolf howled. There was a reply, even more distant. Instinctively, Bogdan Voyvoda's hand moved towards his rifle. But there was no need. That night they would not be troubled by wolf or bear or man.

The night was at its darkest when Ivan first heard the deep bass cry of the kaba gaida calling across the valley. A few hundred yards later, he could see an orange light on the hillside, a fire around which flickering shadows slowly passed. He could see a scattering of rough tents, and sparks that shot up into the night sky like souls released from the earth after long waiting. Over the fire was a spit on which a sheep was impaled. He could smell the meat. Ivan followed Bogdan Voyvoda towards the fire. He could see, now that he was close, the gaida player outside of the circle, the sheepskin bag under his arm, his fingers dancing on the chanter of his pipe, bewildering flurries of ornament. Another man sat on a rock, beating a steady rhythm on a tupan, and some twenty others, hand-in-hand, circled the flames with steady tread. Bogdan Voyvoda held up a hand to indicate Ivan should remain there in the shadows, and then he walked out into the circle. The music stopped immediately. The men let out a cry of welcome. Their Voyvod had returned. They took his pack and his gun, and each in turn embraced him and gave him the kiss of brotherhood. They laid a cloth upon a log, and invited him to sit. They passed around rakiya to drink and waited for their Voyvod to raise a toast to them. Bogdan lifted his cup, spoke a toast softly, and emptied the cup in a single gulp. Once the toast had been drunk, the men began to confer. Ivan remained in the shadows, watching, waiting for the moment when he was summoned.

Not long after Bogdan Voyvoda called to him, and Ivan emerged into the light of the fire. He was embraced by each of the men in turn, Bogdan Voyvoda last of all. They drank a further toast, and then food was passed around. Ivan fell upon it, tearing the flesh of the sheep from the bone. The men all ate in silence. Then, when they were finished, the gaida player took up his pipes, the tupan player lifted his drum onto his knee, and the men rose to dance. Ivan, however, remained where he was. 'You will dance?' the Voyvod asked.

'I will not dance until I have avenged my bride.'

'If you do not wish, do not dance,' the Voyvoda said. 'But dancing leavens the soul as yeast leavens the bread.'

Ivan did not reply. He looked down at the earth, listening to the drone from the pipe, the first, unsteady beats upon the drum. The men who were now his companions circled about the fire. Over the hills to the east, the sky was starting to turn red. Ivan took his wedding hat from his head and tossed it into the flames, watching it burn.

11

Three weeks later, he killed his first man. Not a man so much as a child, younger even than he was. The first few days with the haiduti had been uneventful. Ivan spent the time building the strength the illness had taken from him. His new comrades had taken to the mountains for many reasons. Some were there only for adventure, others out of a hatred; there were those who wanted nothing more than to spend their time free from the burden of the plough and the harvest, and those who fled the wolves of poverty that pawed at the thresholds of their houses; others wished only to shed blood and harvest widows' tears. For Bogdan Voyvoda, it was a simpler thing: he was an exile. If he could have returned home, he surely would. And if he had been able to endure year-long the life of prayer and piety in the monastery outside of Skopje, he would have settled for this. But God remained silent, a poor companion, and Bogdan Voyvoda found himself without a home either in the world of the spirit or in the world of men. The hillsides were a place of last resort.

Ivan kept his distance from the other men. He did not join in when they danced the horo, nor did he respond to their gestures of friendship. He was willing to do everything his Voyvod and his standard-bearer—a thin and anxious man called Boyko—asked of him; but he would not dance or sing or even smile. At night, he lay awake looking at the stars and dreaming of the suffering he would cause the Pasha's son, when he met with him again.

Yet the Pasha's son was already long gone, called away the previous autumn to Constantinople on business, taking his bride with him. There in the city, without the fear some idiot villager would seek revenge for taking what was his by right, he moved through a world of gold and fountains and sweetmeats and pleasures that the villagers of Gela could never imagine. Stoyanka, a prisoner of this luxury, spent her days sewing and gazing out of the window over the city and the sea, enduring the clumsy attentions of the Pasha's son in the evenings, attentions made bearable only because her husband was an unskilled lover and, as frequently as not, his appetite and enthusiasm outstripped his self-control, so that he spilt himself on the silken bedsheets before he had even forced himself inside her.

When Ivan was strong enough, some time towards the summer festival of Petrovden, Bogdan Voyvoda sent him on what should have been a straightforward mission: to accompany Boyko and three others on a raid upon a poor and ill-guarded merchant party on the road down from the mountains to Stanimaka, and to seize all that they could carry in gold and goods, so that they would be able to buy food.

The first part of the plan went well. They crossed the hills on foot and came to the pre-agreed place. There they waited by a cluster of rocks that provided good cover, overlooking the road. After several hours, they peered through the rocks and saw the small party of travellers approach. Only three horses: mounted on the foremost was a poor-looking merchant, his son riding behind him on the same animal, and behind them two other horses, riding abreast as the road was a little wider than usual at that point. On the horses were two armed guards, the kind of paid hands who never put up much of a fight, who have no reason for loyalty or bravery, but only want to earn a few coins so that they might be able to fill their bellies. Each of the horses had slung over its back a merchant's bag. Boyko gave a signal, and the five haiduti emerged from the rocks, firing their guns over the heads of the party. They would have spared the guards, had the guards not been foolish enough to raise their weapons and take aim. Each met with a bullet in the chest. They fell from their horses, and the horses bucked in wild panic, scrambling down the hill to stand restlessly by the banks of the river. The merchant, seeing he was now unguarded, pulled a revolver from his belt, hesitated and then let the gun fall to the ground. His horse came to a halt in the middle of the road. Boyko, Ivan and another of the haiduti surrounded the man and his son with their rifles. The two others dragged the corpses of the guards down to the river, where they pushed them out into the stream. They returned to the track with the two horses.

'Dismount,' ordered Boyko.

The merchant and his son dismounted. One of the robbers took the reins of the horse. Boyko looked at the animals with approval. Three horses would fetch a reasonable price. Or, if this failed, they would make reasonable eating.

'Take off your clothes,' Boyko said.

The merchant hesitated, but the standard-bearer pointed his gun at him. 'Take off your clothes,' he repeated.

The merchant started to strip. 'And you,' Boyko snapped. The boy began to blub softly, but he too took off his clothes, until father and son were standing naked in the road. Boyko nodded to Ivan, who picked up the clothes. They were not expensive, but the quality was good enough.

Boyko looked about him. Time was short, and although the road was quiet, there was no guarantee that nobody else would pass by. 'You are going to Stanimaka?' he asked the merchant.

'Yes.'

'Then go,' the haidut said.

'But our clothes?'

'Be grateful you still can walk,' Boyko replied. 'And make

sure you get to Stanimaka before dusk, or you may freeze your balls off.'

The merchant looked at his son. 'Come,' he said, 'let us go.' But the boy did not respond. He was staring at the rough ground, shaking with anger and humiliation.

'Come,' said the merchant.

The boy looked up, and his eyes met Ivan's. They were perhaps no more than two years apart, Ivan being the older: the boy was more or less the age Ivan had been when he had taken Stoyanka's posy. Then the boy hurled himself at Ivan and threw him to the ground. Ivan wrestled with him for a moment until he was on top of him, straddling the boy's naked body. He pulled the gun from his belt.

The father lunged, but stumbled as a bullet from Boyko's gun entered his cheek. He fell to one side. When he heard Boyko's shot, Ivan's finger tightened on the trigger of his own pistol. The boy spasmed beneath him, gurgled, and then was still. Boyko fired again, to finish off the father. Ivan looked at him. 'Come, ride behind me,' Boyko said. 'We must go.'

But Ivan was transfixed by the body beneath him, by the sheer weight of the fact of death, by the strangeness of that magical transformation in which, in a moment, a person becomes a corpse. He was listening to the rage that ran through his body, and for a moment he thought to himself: yes, this is beautiful.

Boyko mounted the merchant's horse and motioned to Ivan to climb up behind him. He indicated to the other haiduti that they too should mount. They did so, two riding upon the larger of the two remaining horses, and one upon the other. Then they rode back to the encampment.

12

As the storks began preparing for their long journey to the south, the thoughts of the haiduti started to turn towards winter. Boyko planned to return, as he always did, to his natal village, and there spend the cold months in hiding. Some intended instead to head to the cities where they would make what living they could, keeping as far as possible from the eyes of the state. Bogdan Voyvoda's thoughts turned to Skopje and the long, barren nights in his monastery cell. And Ivan too began to reflect upon those interminable cold months when life hiding out in the hills would no longer be possible. To return to Gela would be too painful to bear. How could he look again on the village where, had things been otherwise, he would now be living as a man, alongside Stoyanka, his first child—a son, or maybe a daughter—already born? He did not want the killing season to end. He did not want to sit out the winter in inaction.

He had killed again that summer, four times, and the bitterness that had been seeded on the night of Stoyanka's abduction continued to grow. Each evening, he brooded as he looked into the fire; and it was as if Ivan managed through his brooding to swing the mood of those men, men who were lords only of themselves, who recognised no higher authority than the band of which they were a part, not even God, men whose ferocity had, until not long before, been tempered with the possibility of kindness. Although he was young and with little experience and of no rank, Ivan's bitterness seemed to spread to encompass the entire band. By the day of Golyama Bogoroditsa, the day upon which, the year before, Ivan's father had made offerings to the Virgin so he might be restored to health, the mood of the band had soured. There was little dancing in the evening, and no song. Bogdan Voyvoda was increasingly preoccupied.

Trees started to drop their leaves and the haiduti began to make their way to the places where they would overwinter, like storks or swallows. Bogdan Voyvoda invited Ivan to accompany him to Skopje, to the monastery.

Ivan agreed. Where better than a monastery for bitterness to suppurate, for hatred to be added to hatred, for anger to be distilled?

13

As winter approached, Bogdan Voyvoda and Ivan travelled west through the hills to Bansko, where Father Paisii wrote his history, and from there over the mountains to arrive in Skopje on the eve of Andreevden. They were assigned to their cells and took up the robe; and Ivan became a monk.

Bogdan Voyvoda was accustomed to spending the winter months in bleak quietude, performing such tasks as were necessary, but shunning prayer and the consolations of the liturgy in the small monastery church. He preferred not to spend long hours in conversation with a God who did not see fit to reply. When he first came to the monastery, he attempted to pray with all of his heart and all of his mind, but his prayers spiralled up into the darkness of the winter night and no response came from on high. For all he knew, they were still there, those early mutterings, travelling through black darkness of space like poor, solitary birds blown off course by heavy winds, wandering across the endless ocean until they dropped, exhausted, into the dark swelling nothingness below them. After the first few winters, being a practical mountain man, Bogdan prayed less and less. For the winter months, he simply waited, as the whole world waited under its blanket of snow.

When he was a boy, an old man in Bogdan's home village of Stoikite had told him that if one met God upon the road, one should greet Him and offer Him hospitality; but that if He proved poor company, one should waste no further time with

Him. Bogdan Voyvoda had always remembered that. And poor as his own company was, the company of God seemed all the poorer. He took solace instead in the scant friendship offered by a small fox that appeared one morning by the window of his cell, shivering in the cold. He fed the creature scraps, and it returned the following morning. By the time of Koleda, the fox would allow him to stroke the orange fur of its back. This closeness and this friendship lent a little warmth to those cold months.

Meanwhile Ivan dressed in black, his beard long, and he woke each dawn with prayers on his lips. He seemed to take to life in the monastery so naturally that one would have thought he was made for it. He prayed and worked and intoned the liturgy with the devotion of the perfect novice. He rose early and retired late. He did not smile unbefittingly, or joke with the other younger monks. He kept his gaze lowered and was obedient to his superiors. But the God to whom he prayed was not the God who lays the weary traveller down and blesses His people in peace, whose mercy endureth forever, who marks the fall of every shivering sparrow in the cold mountain snow; instead, He was the God who smites with the rod that is His hand upon the waters which are in the river, that the rivers shall be turned to blood; He was the God who is the bringer of pestilence, who cuts the people off from the earth, from whom wrath is poured out without quenching, through whom the plague is begun. Ivan prayed intensely, unceasingly, so that this God might rain down sickness and misery upon his enemies.

In this way, throughout the winter months Ivan stored up hatred like grain for planting in the coming spring. Every moment, whether awake or asleep, he was accompanied by the thunderous torrent of blood pulsing in his ears, the sound of a fury not yet ready to be unleashed. He spoke his rage to God, but in the presence of all others was silent.

The new year came, and as the weeks passed, the first signs of spring appeared. The fox came less often to Bogdan's window, and the Voyvod started to look anxiously to the trees for the appearance of the buds that would mean his departure. The snows shrank back from the valleys, although they still clothed the peaks in white, and the hills started to sound with the trickling of snowmelt and the tentative songs of small birds. Bogdan realised that it would soon be time for him to leave, and he went to speak with Ivan. 'It is spring,' he said. 'I am returning to the mountains.'

The robes of the monk hung about Ivan's body so naturally that Bogdan half-assumed that he would remain there in the monastery. His face was already like the faces of the saints that stared out from the icons, their eyes sunken and steady, their beards straight, their mouths turned down at either corner in an expression of pious sorrow. So when Ivan replied that he would accompany Bogdan to the mountains once more, the Voyvod hesitated with the surprise of it.

'Then come,' Bogdan said after a short pause. 'I will be leaving before dark.'

The Voyvod retired to his cell, unlocked the trunk beneath his bed and removed the rifle that had lain dormant all winter. He took it apart and cleaned it. Then, before stripping off his monk's robe, he went to the window and called for the fox. It came running through the brilliant green of the new grass, and Bogdan tossed some bread from the window. He stroked its fur in farewell, and watched as it trotted back into the forest. Then he went to make his departure known to the brothers who had sheltered them for the winter months. Having done so, he changed into his summer clothes, the clothes of a mountain man, and walking side by side with Ivan, he left the monastery.

14

They headed back towards the east, sharing bread and silence. After several days, they arrived one evening at the appointed place, not far from the grove where the oak trees stood in a circle, exactly as they had stood in the days of Orfei.

Boyko and several of the others were waiting. The encampment was already established, and a fire was blazing. That night, the haiduti ate heartily, renewing old friendships over rakiya and a sheep roasted on a spit. Ivan sat to one side, responding to the greetings of the other men with the curtest of nods.

The remainder of the haiduti trickled back to the camp over the following days. There were two new members of the band, men who, on account of some injustice or another, had left the plough and their families. Another three had died over the winter, one in prison in Stanimaka, one of sickness, and the third in a drunken knife-fight. The gaidar was the last to return, his appearance a week later announced by the bleating of his pipes, like the crying of lost sheep or the lamenting of slaves. The music he brought drove out the last traces of winter chill from the air. That night there was dancing; and the following morning the summer raiding season began.

Ivan lived like this for five years, spending the summer months in the mountains with the haiduti and the winter months in silent prayer in the monastery with Bogdan. As the years passed, he grew both in silence and in savagery, his beard thickening, his body becoming hardened to the dual asceticism of life in the mountains and in the monastery cell.

During the long summers, he hardly spoke to the other men, passing only a few words to Bogdan, to Boyko, to the cheerful gaidar or to any of the others. He was brave but never rash, merciless in his killing but quick and efficient with a knife, obedient to Bogdan without a trace of subservience. As the years passed, Bogdan found himself studying his protégé's grave features as Ivan stared into the night-time fires, or as he huddled in prayer in the monastery, swathed in silence and in black; and the Voyvod wondered what would become of the bridegroom he had met on the road to Trigrad, whom he had counselled to turn tears into bitterness.

In the spring of 1818 Bogdan left the monastery outside Skopje for the final time. He travelled side by side with Ivan to the grove of Orfei; the men gathered as they did every year; the gaidar appeared, his pipes bleating as they came over the hill; there was feasting and dancing; and once again then the raiding season began. Yet before the month was out, Bogdan Voyvoda had departed the earth without any hope of return.

In that year, a few days after the gathering together of the haiduti, news came that a military detachment was passing through that part of the country. The rumour was—and it was no more than a rumour—that the soldiers were many, too many for the haiduti to fight directly; and so after conferring with Boyko, Bogdan Voyvoda told his men to strike camp, intending to make for rockier territory where they would be safe. It was a cool and fragrant night, and overhead the moon—the bandits' sun, they called it—was shining. They passed through the forest, first underneath broadleaf oak and beech, and then through pine woods where nothing grew upon the forest floor, and where even the night birds were silent. They were making for the river, for the place now known as Haidushki Dol, the ford of the bandits, where they planned to cross into the rocky hills beyond.

When they arrived at the ford, the night was already

advanced, and the moon was beginning to sink behind the hills. Bogdan Voyvoda and his men crouched in the forest and looked out across the river. The distance to the trees on the other side was no more than two hundred paces. On the river's southern bank was a path, but the path was deserted. They emerged from the trees cautiously and started to make their way to the river. Holding their rifles over their heads, they stepped into the icy water. It was at the point when the men were half way across the river that from the trees on the far bank appeared thirty or more horses, the riders in shadow so their military apparel could hardly be made out.

The soldiers fired the first shots before the haiduti had even seen them appear. Then there was panic. Several of the men attempted to swim back to the shore from which they had come. Others took up their positions in the cold water, using rocks for cover, and returned fire. Ivan, who was the furthest upstream and who understood that it was futile, slid into the hollow of the river bank where he might not be seen, and waited.

It was over quickly. Ivan watched as Bogdan Voyvoda, wading through the water towards the trees as if he knew that the least terrible thing he could face was death, took first a shot in the arm and then another in the forehead. He fell backwards. His body thrashed for a few moments in the water and he was still, the corpse pulled away into the dark by the swift currents. Several men made it back to the shore. Of these, three—Boyko amongst them—reached the cover of the trees. Those who remained in the river, holding their positions, fell one by one. Ivan pressed himself into the bank and heard the clop of horses' hooves as the troops emerged from the forest. As far as he could tell, the soldiers had sustained not a single loss. He lay there for a long time, shivering with cold, until the soldiers passed on their way.

When Ivan emerged from the river bank, past the corpses of his fallen comrades, the day was growing light. He waded back to the other bank, and clambered out of the water. Boyko and five others came from the forest to meet him. Boyko carried the standard in his hands, and in his eyes were tears.

'Bogdan is dead,' said Boyko.

'I saw him die,' Ivan replied.

'Then we are seven in all.'

Ivan was silent. Then Boyko knelt before him. 'I am grieving,' he said, 'and we are without a Voyvod to lead us. How can I, Boyko, take my Voyvod's place? Ivan, you are the one I wish to lead.'

Ivan put out his hand and took Boyko's. He helped him to his feet. Then he embraced him.

'If you wish it,' he said, 'then I will accept.'

Part Two

The Voyvod

15

The haidut is laughing,
in the hills, the haidut is laughing,
and the wolves are all howling.
On the mountain, the wolves are all howling,
but the haidut is laughing.
In the valleys, the haidut is laughing,
and the sheep are all bleating.
In the meadows, the sheep are all bleating,
but the haidut is laughing.
In the pines, the haidut is laughing,
and the sparrowhawk cries in the clouds,
but nobody hears its warning.
The rivers will run with blood tonight
under a rebel's moon;
black they will run with blood tonight
under the summer moon.

16

First the stories spread through rumour and song, passed from mouth to mouth and village to village: the haidut Ivan of Gela, Ivan Voyvoda, who was without mercy, who could appear in a moment and cut your throat and then be gone without leaving a single footprint. Some claimed that none were safe from him, whilst others said that he killed only those who were rich, or those who wore green. Stories, always stories. Stories that gave rise to more stories, that in turn multiplied and replicated and mutated, spreading like fevers throughout the countryside. There was no telling which were true and which were false; but as the summer months passed, the merchants going through the part of the country became uneasy at the whispered tales told around the village hearths at night.

Then came the autumn, and the trees began to shed their leaves. The haiduti left the hillsides, for in the winter months there is nowhere to hide and little to eat. Ivan took the lonely roads west to Skopje. By the Wolf Days of November, the trees were almost bare of leaves, the hillsides occupied only by shepherds, and Ivan was dressed in his black robes and spending his days in bitter prayer.

It took only three years from the time that Ivan assumed the role of Voyvod for these tales to reach the ears of Sultan Mahmud II. It was 1821, and Sultan Mahmud the Second, heir of the House of Osman, had sat for thirteen uncomfortable years upon the throne. Often, as he looked at his reflection in the glass, contemplating the slow erosion of his territory, he noted how the beard that had once been jet-black was now becoming grey. There can be no worse inheritance than a throne, he reflected. He was forty-two years old. Every day he awoke to news of growing rebellion in the Greek province of Morea, reports of the hungry expansion of Russian power, and of the increasingly fractious Janissary corps, a problem that throbbed away at him like a bad tooth that one day would need to be extracted.

It was July. A deputation of Ottoman officials, heading northwards across the mountains towards the Danube, had been attacked. They had been well-armed, but had been overcome by superior force or superior cunning or both. Their bodies had been left at night in the square of the small town of Dospat. The officials' throats had all been cut. A local man, under threat of torture, had claimed that this was the doing of Ivan Voyvoda. The Sultan read the brief report and gloomily rubbed his face. It was hot, even in the palace, and the air hung heavily, unmoving and suffocating. 'Who is this Ivan?' the Sultan asked.

'I know little about him,' said his advisor, bowing a fraction. 'His name was first heard two or three years ago, but since then it has been spoken more and more. The rumours are that he is gathering a great army. They are talking of insurrection.'

'And am I to rely only on rumours, or do you have anything better to offer?' There was something acid in the Sultan's voice, but he was thinking: what do I ever have but rumours?

His advisor inclined his head, but remained silent.

'If you hear more of this Ivan Voyvoda, report it to me. But in future, I would prefer something of more substance.'

'Are the corpses of your officials not substance enough?' the advisor asked, and immediately realised he was speaking out of turn.

The Sultan gave him a dark look. 'Dismissed,' he said.

The advisor departed. Mahmud walked to the window. It was at times such as this that he found himself longing for a simpler life, a life spent with music and poetry and his beloved calligraphy; yet it was not in the nature of life to be simple. Even the calligrapher, the poet and the musician suffer many trials.

It was not the last that he heard of Ivan. The terrible summer droned on, and the heat and stink of the city began to penetrate every fragrant corner of the palace. Each day there was fresh news of the growing revolt in Greece, and Mahmud felt sometimes as if the empire was slipping through his fingers. When, weary of the Greeks, he turned his attention elsewhere, the bad news from the Rhodope mountains continued to trickle through. The facts were stark: nine officials killed here, another seven there, merchant caravans raided, imperial goods plundered. All these things could be attested. But there were also the rumours and whisperings, the tales of bands of insurgents taking refuge in caves, networks of sympathisers in every village, monastery and church, the constant drip of stories woven from anxious speculation.

By the height of August, the heat was so fierce in the capital that pious old women were dying in the streets on their way to say their prayers. Mahmud closed his doors and hoped that the coming winter would cool the ardour of his subjects. As for the Ivan Voyvoda, he thought, if he was indeed raising an army, then he would worry about this only when the army appeared in the light of day. There were enough real armies to fret over without also worrying about the invisible ones. But the Sultan worried all the same; and, in an attempt to soothe these worries, his thoughts turned, as they often did, to music.

Any day soon, he thought, the Jew will arrive. That, at least, will provide some relief from the endless cycle of wars and rumours.

17

In truth, however, the rumoured army consisted only of some twenty-five men, with Ivan as their head and the faithful Boyko as standard-bearer. And yet, they were fearsome enough, these haiduti—more terrible, certainly, than in the days of Bogdan. Whilst Bogdan had been a reluctant exile in the mountains, who robbed, when he did, as much for survival as for the pleasure of it, Ivan was driven by the unceasing rage that thundered in his blood like a fever.

Later tradition in those parts would make Ivan a hero of the poor and the scourge of the rich, a bringer of a harsh but necessary justice. But it was simpler than this: the poor had little he could take, and the haiduti relied upon the villagers for trade, for places to shelter in the winter, for food. Why steal from those who have little worth stealing? Why poison the well from which you must drink? And his rage was directed elsewhere. Until he could avenge himself by spilling the blood of the Pasha's son, he would not be content; yet the Pasha's son was far off in Constantinople, and so the rage continued to shudder through him unchecked. He was not indiscriminate, but it is of the nature of rage to spill beyond its proper bounds, so that nobody on the roads, unless they were a poor villager with nothing in their pockets, was entirely safe.

Ivan had shown himself, in his very first year as Voyvod, to be skilled in the art of surprise, a shrewd tactician. He learned quickly how, if one planned with sufficient care, ten men could easily hold fifty or one hundred at bay. When it came to killing, he was quick and brutal. He eschewed many of the cruelties of his time, the slicing and severing, the long drawn-out tortures. He preferred to shoot his victims or slit their throats with the minimum of fuss, a mercy not born out of some latent kindness, but rather because the more quickly one kills, the more one can kill. So Ivan killed repeatedly and ruthlessly, as if the blood of his victims might, as the Blood of Christ was said to do, wash away the sins and the sorrows of the world, so that everything could be made pure and bright again.

If the gaidar still played his pipes in the evenings as they sat by the fire in their mountain encampment—he had been one of the few who had survived the massacre at the ford—and if there were still those who danced the horo around the flames, the encampment had a less joyful air than in the time of Bogdan. Ivan never joined in the dancing. He said little, allowing Boyko to act as his mouthpiece. He rarely looked his men in the eye, except when he toasted them around the fire, raising his glass of rakiya.

It was during his fourth summer as Voyvod, three years after the death of Bogdan and his ninth year in the mountains, that Ivan went off alone. It was a fine summer evening when the grass was still singing with crickets, and some memory provoked Ivan to return to the cave where he had first met with Bogdan, as if he hoped that he might be able to retrace his steps not only that far, but also back from the cave to the village, back through the long winter of burning fever, back beyond the bridge where he had stood in front of the horses, to the night before the wedding, and even further back, to the point at which he had plucked Stoyanka's posy from her hand and placed it in his hat, and she had smiled and laughed, her blue eyes clear and filled with joy; as if the past was not really past and could be rolled up and folded away, to be unfolded again, but differently. And so he set off towards the gorge, and as the sky darkened he allowed his footsteps to follow the track, letting his feet remember where his mind failed, to bring him back to that point when he met with the Voyvod, when he was still dressed in the costume of a groom.

He reached the cave early in the morning, climbed up to the entrance and crawled inside. It was pitch black. He could hear the sound of the dripping water, as he had heard it all those years before. He crawled back out into the moonlight and took a few dry leaves and some sticks. Then he removed the flint from his pouch and struck it until the spark took flame. He blew on the flame so that the leaves caught fire, and then he fed the tiny fire with kindling. When he had done this, he took a bundle of sticks and, clutching it in his fist, he thrust the end into the flames. When the torch was burning well, he got to his knees again and crawled back through the opening to the cave.

Inside, he looked around the chamber, his torch flickering, listening to the trickle of water. There was something white in the corner of the cave, and he crouched down to take a closer look. It was a square of cloth, already beginning to rot, and soiled by the droppings of bats. He recognised it immediately: his wedding handkerchief. Ivan picked it up and lifted it to his face, smelling it. It smelled only of dampness and decay.

He took the handkerchief and crawled back into the night. Then he sat overlooking the road, the torch in one hand and the piece of cloth in the other. He sat there for a long while, listening to the calls of night birds. Then he held the cloth to the flame. It was damp, and lit only with difficulty. Grey, wet smoke curled up into the night sky. Orange flames crawled across the white fabric, turning it to black. He held it until his fingers were burning, then he dropped it onto the stones. The final corner he crushed with his foot. He extinguished the torch and looked up to the sky where the river of the Milky Way was agitated by swarms of shooting stars.

18

Several months before Ivan's return to the cave where he first met with Bogdan, Solomon Kuretic was standing at the window and watching the silken back of the Sultan's emissary disappear down the steps. His long fingers caressed the window-frame and he looked out into the pale April light, hung with mist, that made Vienna—a city more in love with her own image than any other on earth—seem uncommonly modest, to the point of coyness. Overhead he saw a flight of ducks passing, heading in clattering formation for the Danube. The emissary climbed into the coach and was gone. In Solomon's hand was the letter, marked with the Sultan's seal.

Solomon turned from the window and sat down in the chair. He lifted his guitar from its case and, plucking clear bell-like harmonics, coaxed it into tune. He ran through several scale passages to ease his fingers back into the discipline. He had not played for a whole week, and could feel the stiffness already beginning to creep in. He started with an easy study, the one that he had written as an exercise for his teacher, Toepfer, a piece that charmed without ever demanding too much, either from the player or from the listener. Then he rippled through a series of arpeggios of increasing speed and brilliance. When he came to a halt, he sensed there was somebody standing inside the doorway behind him. He looked round. It was Clara.

'So you are going?' she said. She stepped towards him. Solomon thought she looked radiant this morning. Her cheeks were pink and her shoulders bare. The high waistline of her dress accentuated her breasts.

'I am going,' he said.

'For how long?'

'Two years, perhaps.'

Clara came to stand directly before him. She studied his face for a few moments. 'You are going alone?' she asked. It was not so much a question, but a statement of a fact already established.

'I am going alone,' he agreed.

She pulled a chair close and sat down, so he was just an arm's length away, then she smoothed the fabric of her dress over her knees. 'They say the women in Constantinople are beautiful,' she said.

'Perhaps,' Solomon replied, his fingers gently stroking the guitar strings so they whispered with sound. Outside another flight of ducks was going past, or the same ducks heading in a different direction.

'I will probably marry,' she said, twisting her long curls around her fingers.

'Most probably.'

'And the man I marry will be a scoundrel.' She smiled momentarily at the thought.

'Many are.'

She looked to one side, out of the window. 'But,' she added, 'at least he will not desert me.'

Solomon glanced at Clara. She was right. He would not desert her. No sane man would; but the moment he had been offered the possibility of an appointment in the court of Mahmud II, he knew he would leave everything—Vienna, his friends, his family, his beloved teacher, even Clara—just to set eyes on the city of Constantinople. The reasons for his longing were ill-formed and inchoate. They were born in the same place that his love of music was born, that obscure place low in the gut where reason no longer has any hold. He would probably be less happy for it, rather than more; but happiness was not all in life. It seemed strange to him that anybody could be happy settling for something as insubstantial as happiness. To leave Clara was madness, and yet he had given his word, the emissary had left, and here she was, sitting before him, her pale grey eyes on him. She will not marry a scoundrel, he thought. She will marry a schoolteacher or a priest. He will be kind and without passion. And she will long for her dear departed Solomon for the rest of her days. Then he checked himself. For perhaps she would find another, with passion and hunger, as he had been passionate and hungry. That would be the worst: the thought that he was merely preparation for a greater passion to come.

Clara's thoughts flowed in a simpler, less turbulent fashion as she looked away from Solomon to gaze out of the window over the city. Solomon was leaving. And if there would be others, for now there was only Solomon. She didn't want to cry. Not whilst he was still here, beautiful and pale and worried, his guitar in his lap. She leaned forwards and took his hands in her own. 'Play for me, Solomon,' she said.

'What shall I play?' Solomon was almost stammering, and the pathos of it made Clara flush with pleasure.

'Whatever you wish. Just play.'

So Solomon cradled the guitar in his arms. He closed his eyes, and rested his left hand on the fingerboard. The right hand hovered by the sound-hole. He ran his thumb lightly over the strings, to test them once again—the lowest string was flat, and he tuned it up a fraction. Then he started, a waltz in D, slow and grave. When he came to the end, he did not hesitate or glance up, but instead modulated into A, in which key he played two pieces by Aguado. He then changed into E and played one of his own compositions, a lament that Clara found (although she had never confessed this) somewhat dreary, but one that never failed to bring tears to Solomon's own eyes. Finally, he played the *Grand Solo* Opus 14, by the incomparable Spaniard Ferdinand Sor, a piece that he had learned from a French edition. Clara slipped out of the room before Solomon finished playing. Solomon did not even notice her go. When he came to the end of the piece, he let the final chord resound until he could not hear it any longer. Then he placed his hand flat over the sound-hole and opened his eyes.

Clara was gone. He put the guitar in its case, rose from his seat and walked to the window. The mist was beginning to lift from the city of Vienna. Solomon stood by the window and dreamed of the East.

19

Solomon Kuretic had been born in Vienna, the son of two Croatian Jews who had fled to the city in 1783, after Josef II issued his proclamation of tolerance. Solomon had been schooled in German, and to all outward signs he lived as any other citizen of the city on the Danube. Yet in private, he still celebrated the Passover, and his body bore the scar where his skin had been removed, marking him once and forever as a Jew. The first time Clara had seen the scar, she had almost screamed, and yet she had become accustomed to it before long, there was much else to admire about Solomon, after all, particularly when naked.

It had been Clara who had led him to the guitar. One evening, seven years before, Solomon had attended a concert given in the city by Karl Toepfer, the actor, guitarist and philosopher. During the performance, he had been spellbound by the sweetness of the instrument, and had rashly said as much, on his departure from the concert hall, to the young lady with dark hair and grey eyes who was standing to his side. Clara had smiled and blushed, and confessed that Toepfer was her cousin. She would, she had said, be delighted to introduce them.

Toepfer took on Solomon as a pupil. He progressed rapidly, and as he did so, he won Clara's affections. By the time Solomon was performing his debut on the concert stage, playing several compositions written by his teacher and an arrangement of his own of a theme by Mozart, he and Clara were lovers.

It was in 1821 that an emissary from the Sultan attended one of Solomon's concerts. Tone-deaf himself, the emissary had been requested to seek out musicians to be brought to Constantinople to contribute to Mahmud's reforms in the art of music. Seeing that the audience were impressed by the guitarist's art, he went backstage to speak to Solomon. The letter of invitation followed a few weeks later.

When the news of the commission got out, the local newspapers assumed that nobody would be foolish enough to leave Vienna—which, as everybody knows, is the most beautiful city in the world—for a place such as Constantinople. There were jokes that the Turks, having failed to capture the city in its entirety, were now attempting to take the citizens one by one, starting with the very best. However, when it became clear that Solomon had agreed that he would indeed leave for Constantinople, the same papers asked sourly what else one could expect from a Jew and a turncoat, and they said that the Turks could have Solomon Kuretic, for all they cared.

When Solomon read those newspaper reports, he smiled to himself, a smile without pleasure. Then, as he always did when he was perplexed, he picked up his guitar, and he played it until the stillness settled again in his heart.

20

Solomon Kuretic departed for Constantinople in the late spring, not long after Easter, when the city parks were filled with flowers; and if the pain of leaving Clara continually nagged at him as the carriage rumbled away from Vienna, he had his guitar to console him, and the thought of dark-eyed Turkish women made languid with opium. First he headed east to Bratislava and from there to the cities of Buda and Pest, cities of beautiful women, where the river turned south. He was reluctant to leave the river he had known since birth. He had made excellent progress since Vienna, and was not expected in the border town of Palanka until several weeks later, so he lingered too long by the river, finding lodgings on the southern side in Pest. He spent his days in the coffee houses, dreaming through the mist and the fog, and playing his guitar to win the affections of several women who, he ardently hoped, might take his mind off the memory of Clara. He performed once on the concert stage in the city, and the performance was well received. Sometimes in the evenings he sat alone, looking out of his window over the river, and read the verses from his Bible with its square letters. But after several weeks, he realised that he should be on his way again, and that he would have to leave the river. The only good road led east, for the road to the south was difficult on account of the fighting in Serbia; and so he headed towards Wallachia and there turned south, rejoining the river just north of the town of Palanka.

He had discussed the route in detail with the emissary in

Vienna. It was agreed that he would be met by an official in Palanka, a man by the name of Mehmet Bey. From that point onwards, the emissary said, he would need to travel with a convoy, to ensure his safety. Mehmet Bey would see to it that he was well looked after.

By the time he set eyes on the Danube again, spring seemed to have given way to summer and the river, which had been swelled by the snowmelt, was now subsiding; and yet it was still broad and wide and magnificent, more magnificent, even, than in Vienna or where it ran between the twin cities of Buda and Pest. It was a river that could bring tears to the eyes of a traveller, a river that seemed, in certain light or when there was a faint mist that obscured the far bank, more like an ocean.

Until the point at which he reached the northern borders of the Bulgarian provinces, Solomon had travelled in considerable luxury. The Sultan's emissary had ensured that he receive a generous sum to cover his expenses. But in the wretched village on the northern shore of the river, opposite Palanka, there were no boats to be chartered, and thus he was forced to travel on the leaking passenger ship with the merchants and traders. It was a large and ugly brute of a boat. There were two classes of tickets for the crossing. Those purchasing the cheaper tickets went below decks, where they took their chances with the fetid air, the rats and the swilling water that came in through the leaky boards. The more expensive tickets enabled one to travel on deck, out in the open, and it was here that Solomon elected to suffer the passage over the river. But he was jammed in between a seller of sheep-skins that had only recently been removed from their former owners, and had not yet been properly cleaned, and a man transporting hundreds of brightly coloured birds in cages. He hunched up on the deck, hugging the waist of his guitar case as if it was a woman, and waited for the journey to end.

On his arrival at Palanka, things were not much better. He made himself known at the customs house, a cramped building where there was complete uproar, with countless people coming and going, clerks and officials seated at small desks filling in the papers that were stacked in great piles in every corner of the room, money changing hands, shouts and curses, and—from somewhere outside the door that led to the back of the building—the cries of a man being flogged. A smuggler, perhaps, between each blow telling himself how lucky he was to have escaped only with a flogging.

Solomon went from desk to desk, asking for assistance, but nobody in the customs house spoke German, nor did they speak French, which he also knew passably well. Every time he managed to push though the crowds to make himself known at one of the desks, he only had to stutter a few words to find himself shooed away with irritation whilst others pushed in front of him, waving money and documents and curses. He left the customs house and, breathing deep of the air outside, swore to himself in Yiddish. A man in official dress overheard him, and turned and smiled. 'By your dress, you appear to be a gentleman, Sir,' he said, 'although by your language you are not.' The language the man spoke was also Yiddish, although it was a different dialect, and the vowels and consonants sounded thick and strange.

'You speak my language?'

The other man smiled at him. 'What brings a wandering Jew to Palanka? You have a zither, I see.'

'A guitar. I am here on official business.'

The other man looked interested. 'Official business?'

'I am on a commission from the Sultan. I have been told to ask for Mehmet Bey.'

The official grinned. 'Mehmet Bey,' he said, 'is not a good man. First he will help you, then he will rob you. But first, of course, he will help you, and it seems to me that you are a man in need of help. So there is little that you can do other than take the inevitable robbery in good heart when it comes.'

'Can you bring me to him?'

The official shouted out something in a language Solomon did not understand, and in a moment a small boy appeared. He had only one arm, and a surly lip. The official whispered something to the boy, and then turned to Solomon. 'You must go with him. He will take you to Mehmet Bey.'

21

Mehmet Bey lived in a house a little way up the hill from the customs post. Solomon followed the boy, who took him as far as the door and then stood, looking up at the foreigner sulkily, his hand out, waiting for a tip. Solomon gave him a few small coins, but the boy just stood still and so Solomon added to them. The boy shrugged, closed his fist around the coins, and called out, 'Mehmet Bey!' Then the boy turned and jogged back down the road towards the harbour.

The door opened, and sweet-smelling smoke came from inside. Mehmet Bey stood just over the threshold, a short man, dressed with precision, with a broad face that seemed as if it might be fixed in a perpetual smile, but a smile without much in the way of merriment. It was the smile of a merchant. 'Welcome,' he said, in German. 'You are the musician?'

Solomon confirmed the fact.

'You must come in, we have been waiting for you.' Solomon was relieved that this man spoke his language, and he entered the house, stooping as he went through the low door. Mehmet Bey inclined his head at Solomon's feet, and the visitor understood that he should remove his shoes. He placed the guitar down, took off his shoes and then, unshod, Mehmet Bey ushered him towards a sofra, a low table, surrounded by cushions. The house had an air of slightly seedy elegance. Mehmet Bey invited him to sit and called into the darkness of the back room. 'I presume you drink coffee,' he said to his guest. 'Vienna, I believe, is famous for its coffee houses, although I have not seen them myself. I hope that the coffee here is adequate.'

Solomon smiled, but the smile was strained. There was a sweet smell in the room that unsettled his stomach. Mehmet Bey sat opposite him. 'You are travelling a long way to play music for the Sultan,' he said. 'I trust that he is rewarding you well.'

'The Sultan is generous,' Solomon agreed.

'Perhaps he is. Tell me, friend, how generous is he?'

'Sufficiently,' said Solomon.

'Generous enough, I should imagine, to allow you to be generous in turn.'

'I have nothing to complain of.'

Mehmet Bey leaned back on his cushions. 'What fortune,' he said, 'to have nothing to complain of. I, on the other hand, have a hard life. Every day I work for the Sultan, but I am not skilled in the art of music, I am not an artist or a poet. God distributes his gifts unevenly amongst men, and there are some who are made for beauty and idleness, whilst others are made for hard work. Our Sultan, you understand, loves fine things. He loves calligraphy, beautiful verses, paintings, filigreed screens of marble. And those of us whom God has not seen fit to bestow with such gifts of skill, he rewards us less handsomely.'

Mehmet Bey could, Solomon judged, have gone on in this vein for quite a while, were he not interrupted by an astonishingly beautiful servant girl who came in on bare feet with a gold tray upon which were cups of coffee and a small heap of sweetmeats. Mehmet Bey followed her movement across the room with his eyes, and reached out to brush her leg with his fingers as she placed the tray down on the sofra. Then he turned to his guest. The girl left the room without making a sound. 'Please, although I am poor, I will serve you as best I can. And whilst we drink, we will talk business. There is a convoy leaving for

Constantinople later today. You will travel with them. They are under armed guard and you will be safe. I will send a letter ahead to let the Sultan know that I have discharged my duty to you. But first, please drink.'

As they drank coffee, Solomon tried to make small-talk, or at least to find out where Mehmet Bey had travelled to learn such good German. Yet Mehmet Bey was not a man given to self-disclosure, and he ignored any of Solomon's questions that looked as if they were in danger of penetrating beyond the perpetually smiling mask. After coffee, Mehmet Bey excused himself, saying that he had some business to attend to, reassuring his guest that he would return soon. Solomon lay back on the soft cushions, and despite himself, he fell asleep.

He was woken a couple of hours later by Mehmet Bey, who said that all was in order and that the convoy would be leaving within the hour. The coffee tray had been taken away and the sofra folded and placed by the wall. 'Before you leave,' the official said, 'perhaps you could play for me a little of the music for which the Sultan sees fit to pay you so handsomely.'

Solomon did not want to play for this man, but Mehmet Bey insisted. So he took his guitar from its wooden case, put it on his lap, and caressed the strings. Then he closed his eyes and played Sor's *Variations from the Magic Flute*. When he finished, he opened his eyes and he saw, in the dark of the doorway, the serving girl peering at him, and smiling. When she caught his eye, she slipped away.

Mehmet Bey looked at Solomon coolly. 'You are not wholly without skill,' he said. 'Come, we must go. But first let me detain you with a request. I am a poor man, and I have offered you the gift of hospitality. If you would like to recompense me, then I would be very grateful.'

Solomon hesitated.

'Just a small gift, for a poor man without talent.'

The guitarist reached into his pocket and took out his purse. He removed several coins and placed them into Mehmet Bey's hands. His host looked disappointed. 'Ah, you are on commission from the Sultan, and I am just an official. Please, my friend, a little more.'

Solomon thought of the Yiddish-speaking official at the custom's house, and then reminded himself that he needed Mehmet Bey's help, so he added a little money. His host asked a further time, and once again Solomon gave him more coins. This went on for some while, until Mehmet Bey finally let up, by which time Solomon had paid him as much as it had cost to spend several nights in the guest-house in Buda. But, he consoled himself, at least he had been robbed in daylight, with his own full agreement. Then Mehmet Bey—looking genuinely satisfied—took him back to the marketplace, and from there to the small caravanserai not far from the banks of the Danube, where he introduced him to the merchants with whom he would be travelling all the way to Constantinople.

22

They set out late that afternoon and spent the night in the village of Rasovo. They were up before dawn the following day, Solomon mounted on the back of a bad-tempered bay horse. He was not entirely inexperienced in riding, but he sat uncomfortably on the Ottoman saddle, and the miles passed slowly. The convoy consisted of three parties of traders, each guarded by five soldiers, and several, like him, who were travelling alongside for protection. There must have been over thirty in all, a substantial group, almost a small army, and every one of them was armed. Even Solomon, who had in his life wielded nothing more dangerous than a guitar, was compelled to take up a rifle. The man who gave it to him, who was in charge of the convoy, did not see fit to instruct him in its use, and had Solomon protested that he did not know what to do with it, he would have been met not so much with ridicule as with incredulity, for no man in those parts was ignorant of the use of a rifle. The rifle chafed against him where it was slung on his back, and it made Solomon uncomfortable. He would gladly have thrown it off and abandoned it entirely. Knocking against his back, it felt like a continual reminder that death was not far away.

His travelling companions were courteous and generous towards him. Word had got round that he was on a special commission from the Sultan, and he was well treated. Nobody wished to be subject to Mahmud II's wrath. Yet he did not share a single word with any of the men in the convoy. The language of the convoy was a kind of camp-language, a mix of Bulgarian and Turkish with a smattering of Greek and a few words of several obscure and now largely obsolete local dialects thrown in. Solomon did not understand any of it. He smiled when the others smiled at him, he looked horrified when they looked horrified, he laughed when they laughed, and when they bristled with rage he looked at the ground, for he was not given to rage. On several occasions, in the evenings, if they were not too tired, and as they were sitting by the fire in some poor peasant's house, they would ask him to play, and he would take his guitar from its case, the cedar top reflecting the flames, and he would play by heart the pieces he loved. At these times, perhaps warmed by rakiya or by thick, sweet local wine, sated by the rough bread and mutton stew provided by his hosts, surrounded by these men whose names he did not even know, when he sat by the fire and his fingers coaxed beautiful music from the guitar, he almost felt happy; and Vienna, Clara—even, as the days passed, the Danube—all seemed as far away as childhood dreams, or stories told by others. As he played, it seemed as if there was nothing more to life than this endless road, a rifle at his back, surrounded by a babel of incomprehensible tongues, this continual round of sunrises and sunsets over the slowly changing terrain.

The route taken by the convoy was a long one. They were merchants who travelled almost every day of their lives, and they made steady progress without being in any kind of hurry. They headed south first of all, then turned east to the town of Vratsa. After two nights in Vratsa, resting the horses, they travelled on through Rumelia to the city of Sofia, the city of wisdom. There they rested for five days, five days during which Solomon saw more of folly than of wisdom, and during which he attended the synagogue, an experience that left him melancholy and dissatisfied. From Sofia they continued southwards, and then they took the road over the mountains through Razlog and the village of Dobrinishte to the settlement of Dospat, where again they rested for two days, all the time buying and selling, buying and selling. Once they entered the mountains, the men laughed and joked less, and were more careful to arrive at their boarding places before the sun set. The ride was long and tedious, sometimes across broad meadows or along the banks of streams, and sometimes following treacherous paths that wound along the sides of the mountains, so that at every step Solomon found himself worried that the horse would stumble and that he—or his guitar, which was strapped to the back of his saddle—would go plummeting down into the valley to lie at the bottom, broken and useless.

They had been travelling for twenty-three days when they rose one morning in the village of Teshel, just north of Haidushki Dol where Bogdan Voyvoda had fallen, and took the road east, making for Shiroka Luka. The merchants were in a gloomy mood. For the previous few days there had been heavy rains, mostly in the night, and the good paths had washed away, so that the horses were compelled to repeatedly pick their way through the forest, or else to clamber over rocks and stones and piles of mud. They had been making slow progress, and the mountains were not a good place to make slow progress. At several points, they needed to walk instead of riding, leading their horses behind them. This inconvenience, along with the natural tensions that arise in a group travelling together for many days, put them all in a poor frame of mind. The villagers who had hosted them for the previous few nights had not helped. They had told stories—stories of which Solomon, being protected by his ignorance of the language, had no inkling—of haiduti and robber-bands, of a man called Ivan who was without mercy; and these stories made the merchants anxious, seeping into their dreams at night so that they cried out and woke unrested. So they rose up early, without pleasure, and headed east of Teshel, and when the road opened out and became better for the riding, Solomon half-dozed on the back of his horse, letting it simply follow the creature ahead. He was like a man suspended between the dream of the past and the dream of the future. Behind him was the elegance of Vienna, with her gardens and her concert halls rippling with applause, with her bodiced women whose breasts rose and fell in time with their breath; in front of him were the gilded domes and minarets of Constantinople, her harbours filled with ships and ringing with the sounds of the music of the Janissary corps. In between was this endless road, this horse that simply put one foot in front of the other, its head down, snorting in complaint.

Both Solomon and his horse were so startled by the first gunshots that they froze on the spot. The convoy was on a narrow path just south of the hamlet of Grohotno and, because it is not possible to remain vigilant all the time, nobody was expecting the attack when it came. There was another volley, and the horses at the front fell to the ground. Solomon's own horse seemed to come to its senses. It turned in panic, but its retreat was blocked by the rest of the convoy. Solomon's first instinct was to turn and grab his guitar case. As he was twisting his waist to put his arms around the guitar, the horse threw Solomon to the ground. He fell, his guitar in his arms, and his forehead struck a stone. Then the dream of the present faded too, the valley disappeared, and Solomon lay on the mountain road, his arms around his guitar case—Clara, he thought, as his eyes closed, had often accused him of loving his guitar more than he had loved her—as if dead.

He was woken by a kick from Boyko, who had led the raiding party. Solomon sat up, still hugging his guitar. His head was pounding. Eight men stood before him, and Boyko was

93

holding a standard in his hand. The grubby flag shuddered in the light breeze. The men all had rifles, some of them two or three to a man, and as Solomon looked around, he saw that the merchants, the soldiers and guards, his travelling companions, were all dead, their bloodied corpses scattered between the river to the West to the rocks to the East. The sun was not even at its zenith. It must have been a quick battle. Those horses that had been spared were now laden with loot. Solomon's rifle had been taken from him. Boyko kicked him again, and indicated that he should get to his feet. Solomon stood and held his guitar to his chest, not looking at the men who surrounded him, waiting for the bullet. He realised now that his pockets had been emptied, that they had taken his purse, his Bible. Next, he thought, they will take my guitar. Then they will take my life.

But they did not kill him, nor did they try to wrest the guitar from him. Instead, they turned him round and then, with a rifle pointed in his back, the small party—eight men, who had defeated a well-armed group of thirty—forced him up the goat track that led away from the road. Why have they spared me? he wondered. Why me, and not any of the others? And for how long?

23

Ivan was not at the encampment when they arrived, so they tied Solomon's hands together and roped him to a tree. They gave him water to drink and left him there, with his guitar by his side, for the rest of the afternoon.

Solomon sat looking out across the hills, smelling the scent of summer flowers as it blew across the meadows, listening to the sound of distant sheep and the voices of the men in the encampment; and for the first time in days, he felt entirely freed from anxiety. It was not that he was foolish enough to believe that, having survived the ambush, he would be released unharmed; it was more that he no longer had any power to act to save himself. He could only wait. And so, with resignation, that is what Solomon Kuretic proceeded to do, looking across the valley, allowing the seconds and minutes to pass.

When the sun dipped out of sight behind the hills, the air became appreciably colder. Solomon shivered. The men were tending the fire some distance off, stoking it to make the flames grow higher, but it was too far away to be of any good to the musician. Several of the men were drunk, and occasionally one came over to stare at him. That was all they did. They stared. They didn't prod him or taunt him or torment him, they just stared.

The sky darkened and the birds took refuge for the night. Solomon was shivering more fiercely now, although he felt curiously calm. His guitar was just out of reach. He was reassured by its presence. The fire lit up the hillside with an orange glow. He watched as the men began cooking the carcass of a sheep over the flames. Solomon could smell meat. Then the gaidar started playing, and he closed his eyes and listened.

He probably slept, or blacked out again. When he opened his eyes, the man he had seen with the standard in his hand, Boyko, was standing before him with a hunk of meat. He pointed to the meat and then to his own mouth. Then he untied Solomon and sat watching him, pointing a pistol at his forehead, as the musician gnawed upon the meat which he held in both hands. After Solomon had finished, and let the bones drop on the ground, Boyko gave him a bottle to drink from and Solomon took a swig. Some kind of fierce spirit or other. It made him wince, but it was warming. All the time, Boyko kept the pistol trained on him, although even if Solomon had run, there would have been nowhere for him to go.

'Boyko,' said Boyko, pointing to himself.

Solomon repeated the word. 'Boyko.'

Boyko smiled, then waved the barrel of his pistol at Solomon's chest questioningly.

'Solomon,' said Solomon. 'Solomon Kuretic.'

Boyko frowned, and then he repeated the sounds, rolling them around his mouth. They sounded more guttural than they did when Solomon spoke them.

Then Boyko leaned forward, still holding the gun. 'Evrein?' he asked.

'I don't understand,' Solomon said.

'Evrein?' he repeated. The word had a bitter edge to it.

Solomon shrugged. But Boyko leaned forwards until his face was no more than a foot away. A third time he asked, 'Evrein?' and he pointed the gun beneath Solomon's jaw.

'He wants to know if you are Jewish.' The voice came from the darkness behind Solomon. The musician looked round. The

German was accented, but it was good. One of the haiduti was standing a little distance away, a middle-aged man who was both tall and handsome, although his hair was starting to turn grey. He had been a merchant in his youth, travelling as far as the Rhine in the North; but having been robbed and lost first his fortune and then his wife, he had eventually returned home and taken to the hills with the rest of the haiduti. He was holding Solomon's Bible in his hand, with its square letters. The Bible was inscribed in German, in the inside cover. It had been given to him as a child in Vienna.

'I am Jewish,' Solomon said. 'I come from Vienna.'

The German-speaker confirmed this to Boyko, who muttered something bitter, and pressed the gun into the place below Solomon's jawbone.

'He says that you are a Christ-killer,' the other man translated. 'And for that he hates you.'

Solomon closed his eyes. 'I am a musician,' he said. He had heard all this before, and it bored him: Christ-killer, child-eater, caster-of-spells, money-lender.

The translator repeated Solomon's words in Bulgarian. Boyko replied gruffly.

'It is because you are a musician,' the translator said, 'that you have been spared.'

Boyko removed the gun and stepped back. The two men conversed for a while. The German-speaker clicked his tongue thoughtfully. Boyko tied Solomon up again. They then started towards the fire.

'What will you do to me?' Solomon asked.

The German-speaker turned back. 'We will wait for the Voyvod,' he said. 'When he returns, if he wants to keep you, he will keep you. If not, he will kill you.'

24

Solomon did not need to wait long. Ivan returned to the
encampment within the hour. The first sign of his arrival was
the gaidar, who ceased playing his pipes. Then Ivan appeared
out of the darkness, on the further side of the hill. As he came
close to the fire, Solomon noticed the grave, bearded face, the
deep-set eyes that had something wild about them. The new
arrival, the Voyvod, spoke with Boyko the standard-bearer, then
he came from the fire to the tree where Solomon was tethered,
accompanied by the German-speaker. He crouched down in front
of the prisoner and looked into his eyes. Solomon looked back,
blinking occasionally. For the first time since his capture, he felt
afraid. And cold, too, with the wind that came across the
hillside. His head throbbed where it had hit the rocks. The
moment he thought of the pain, it came flooding back, and he
winced. He could smell Ivan's breath, and the animal reek
coming off the furs he was wearing. The one who spoke German
muttered something to the Voyvod, who broke his gaze and
turned his head. The two men conversed for a while in Bulgarian.
Then the Voyvod walked over to Solomon's guitar case, which
was lying to his side. He kicked it with his toe, but gently, and
asked the German-speaker something.

'He wants to know what it is,' the German-speaker
translated.

'Tell him it is a guitar.'

The Voyvod looked puzzled.

'Music,' said Solomon.

'Muzika,' the translator said.

'Muzika,' Solomon repeated.

Ivan Voyvoda frowned, and then muttered something else to the translator.

'He says that he wants you to open the case. He wants to see the instrument.'

'You will have to untie me first.'

After a short discussion, Ivan leaned over, and taking a knife cut the ropes that tied Solomon. He said something to the translator, who had taken his pistol from his belt and was pointing it at the musician.

'Open.'

Solomon got to his feet, but he was stiff from long sitting, and he wavered a little, steadying himself by reaching out to the trunk of the tree. Then he undid the latches of the case and opened it. The top of the guitar glowed dull orange.

'Tambura,' said Ivan.

'Kitara,' the translator replied.

Ivan stood over the captive, watching him lift the guitar from its case. As the prisoner picked up the instrument, his hand brushed lightly over the strings, which hummed in the night. The image passed through Ivan's mind, so fleetingly that he hardly noticed it, of a blizzard of yellow blossom.

Solomon stood, holding his guitar in his hand. 'Kitara,' he said, and he smiled.

Ivan did not smile back. He spoke to the translator for a few moments more, then turned and headed back towards the fire. The translator, who was still pointing the pistol at the musician, spoke softly. 'The Voyvod has offered you a wager,' he said.

'What kind of wager?'

'It is simple. He has gone to prepare a place for you by the fire. Tonight, the Voyvod will give you food and drink, and all the hospitality that is proper for an honoured guest. Then he will ask you to play.'

'And the wager?' Solomon said.

'The wager is this. If you play with sufficient skill to ease his suffering, he will spare you. But if your playing does not please him, if it does not still his rage and his pain, he will kill you.'

'If I am to die,' Solomon said slowly, 'how shall I die, and when?'

'Our Voyvod will make sure your death is quick. If you have not succeeded by the time that the sun rises over the hill, then he will plant a bullet here.' The translator gently pressed his gun into the middle of Solomon's forehead. Then he placed it back in his belt and put his arm around the musician. 'But that is for later,' he said. 'For now, let us eat and drink as brothers.'

So the two men went to join the circle by the flames, the tall, pale Jewish musician who held his guitar in his hands, and the merchant who had fallen on hard times; and when Solomon took his seat, the haiduti welcomed him, as if he was already one of their number.

Ivan sat on the far side of the fire, poking at the embers with a stick.

25

Solomon shivered as the haiduti passed around clay cups, glazed with green and filled with rakiya. Ivan Voyvoda offered a toast, raising his cup, and the men all responded, taking care to look each other in the eye in turn. Solomon swallowed the brandy and tried not to wince, but in truth he was not feeling much like feasting.

The German speaker, who only now introduced himself as Asen, and who became increasingly voluble and friendly the more they drank, translated for the musician, and the other men pressed him with questions about life in Vienna, about the women there, and about his music. It would have seemed that the band were a model of hospitality were it not for the fact that hanging over Solomon's head was the threat of death the following dawn. Yet in this respect, he was no different from the others, for whom every day offered the prospect of a new and different death. Solomon was not the only man on that hillside who was living in the shadow of his own destruction, and perhaps it was this, above all, that led to the sense of kinship, even of friendship, that his captors felt towards him.

Whatever the reason, they broke bread together, drank rakiya and wine, feasted on fish pulled from the streams and the rivers—silvered trout that crackled as they cooked on the embers, and on mutton and on blackened peppers that tasted of sun. And although Solomon wanted more than anything to keep his head, so that he might play well—he had played for love before, for the hearts of women, but never for his life—he could not refuse the endless toasting, so that by the time the evening was well advanced, he was singing haidut songs along with the others, accompanied by the gaidar, songs of bold raids, of fallen friends, of hatreds and revenge and of quiet meadows where the trees sang with the sounds of finches and sparrows. And even though he did not know the words, it did not matter. He made up his own words, singing about his home, about the Danube he loved, about Clara, about his childhood, so that had he not been already driven half-mad by his long journey, by the blow to his head, by the fear that was growing inside him moment by moment, by the drone of the pipes and the rough sound of so many men's voices, he might have stepped back and wondered that this was a strange way to spend what could be his final night on earth.

But he sang also because whilst he sang, the moment when he would have to play had not yet come; because whilst he sang, he could imagine that he was simply a traveller enjoying the hospitality of shepherds and villagers, a traveller who might, when the dawn came, depart on the road that led east to Constantinople.

When the moon was high overhead, the singing came to a close. The gaidar ceased playing, and Ivan Voyvoda said something in a low voice, something that made all the men laugh, all except Solomon. Asen did not translate. Solomon was swaying a little, more drunk than he could remember having ever been; and when he managed to focus, he saw that there all of the men were staring at him.

Solomon took the guitar and placed it in his lap. He wrapped his arms about it and closed his eyes. The world was pitching and reeling like a ship. Ivan Voyvoda muttered something else, and this time Asen did translate. 'The Voyvod asks you to play,' he said. 'He asks you to play to ease his suffering heart.'

Solomon ran his fingers along the strings. His pale right hand hovered over the sound hole, his left crouched on the fingerboard. He paused, tested the tuning, and made what adjustments he could; but because of the drink it was hard to be sure whether he was making things better or worse. Then he played a chord—an E minor that set the four open strings thrumming—just to test the sound. He ran through another few chords. Then he looked into the fire.

What can a man play, he wondered, to save his life? And because none of those things he had performed on the concert stage were adequate to the occasion, because an encampment in the Rhodope mountains, surrounded by men who have just slaughtered every last one of your travelling companions, is no place for delicate Viennese waltzes, for the fripperies of the salons of Europe, he simply let his fingers guide him. He played the lightest of passages in harmonics, echoed them on the bass strings, playing in heavy rest-strokes with his thumb, a melody that came to him from nowhere, or perhaps from everywhere, from the long road he had travelled, from his regret at leaving Clara, from the fear that was settling in his belly, coiled like a guard dog only half-asleep, from these hillsides with their gorges and valleys, their upland meadows and rushing streams filled with trout and fringed by green ferns, from the music he had heard played in the houses of peasants along the way, from the sky above with its incomprehensible stars, and from the eyes of the men who sat listening to him, immobile, no longer even passing around the rakiya, but simply listening. The melody inched its way up the stave, fugue-like, repeating each time, but never quite the same, a melody like the river that, as some sage once said, one can never step into twice, but that remains the same river. There were waterfalls of arpeggios, swirling whirlpools of triplets, slow-moving depths on the lower strings, clashes that were only partly resolved before becoming still further clashes, dissonances and tensions and cross-rhythms that built upon each other until Solomon's hands were a blur; but somehow, out of this chaos of notes, the same melody, returning again and again. Then his hands slowed, and his left hand moved up to the top of the fingerboard where the melody appeared once more, modulating into the minor key with such extraordinary sweetness that—had he still been walking in those hills, had he not been torn to pieces by savage women as a punishment for spurning their advances—even Orfei himself would have wept to hear it. Solomon pulled the melody from the guitar in long skeins, drawing it out like silk. And then the tempo quickened, the discords becoming more pronounced, rhythms of the soil and of the rocks and of the trees, uncountable rhythms felt only in the body, beginning to take over. The gaidar smiled and leaned forward. He had heard nothing like this before, and yet it was as if he had always been waiting to hear it. His fingers twitched, following the flood of ornaments and grace notes. Asen leaned back, breathless. Boyko put his face in his hands, for what reason it is impossible to tell. And Solomon played on, as the sparks flew up into the night, and the dead on the hillsides, unseen, clustered around to listen, because it is not every day that you get a concert such as this, and if the dead are not easily roused, they are not entirely intractable; and as the dead assembled, although they could not be seen, the haiduti shivered at their presence and at the strange spell that Solomon was weaving, not a music of the head, nor even of the heart, but of the hands that danced like ghosts in the firelight, the hands and the body and the ancient earth singing through the body and the sinews and the blood.

Then the melody eased, became simple again. Played on the bass strings. Echoed once in the higher register. Again, but more gently, in the bass. And again at the top of the guitar, but in harmonics, clear and pure as a mountain spring, the final note so quiet that it was not certain whether it was played, or simply imagined.

Solomon opened his eyes. His head was pounding and he was damp with sweat. He looked around the fire. Nobody clapped. Nobody moved. Then he saw Ivan Voyvoda: and tears were streaming down the man's face.

The Voyvod rolled his shoulders and cleared his throat. His men turned and looked at him with astonishment, for they had never once seen him weep. He then let his head hang, so that the tears fell into his lap. His verdict was murmured so softly it was almost inaudible. 'The Jew lives.'

26

Solomon started to shudder. Uncontrollable tremors swept repeatedly through his body. The men passed him another cup of rakiya, but it did not still his trembling.

Ivan Voyvoda stood up, wiping the tears from his eyes with his sleeves. His face was pale and grave. He stood by the dying fire and it was as if his heart, his heart that had been a dark and endless hollowness that he had filled and refilled with bitterness without the bitterness ever reaching up to the rim, had now become strange to him: as if at the bottom of everything was not simply darkness twisted together with darkness, but instead a kind of brightness; as if a spring had burst forth in him, falteringly perhaps, the waters of which were clear and cool and peaceful. It was not that the hatred was gone. Ivan could sense it, endless and deep as the night was endless and deep; but at the very centre of things there was something that was not hatred, something that held the darkness at bay. And it was sweet.

Ivan took a blanket. He walked around the fire and with the gentleness of a mother tending her only child he wrapped it around the musician's shoulders. He took the guitar from Solomon's hands and placed it in the case. Then, with an air of great solicitude he led the musician away from the fire, and prepared him a sleeping place in one of the tents. Ivan indicated with broad gestures that Solomon should lie down. He covered him with another blanket, and placed the guitar by his side. The Voyvod left the tent and returned to the fire. Boyko, Asen and the others did not glance up at him, but they were troubled. Something had changed in their Voyvod, with the coming of the Jew who played the tambura; and the thought made them uneasy.

Inside the tent, Solomon shivered underneath the blanket that smelled of sweat and of sheep and of woodsmoke. It took a while for him to get warm, for the coldness of death that had brushed against him to be driven out again by the living pulse of his body. But eventually, he turned to his side, embracing the guitar, and fell asleep like that, hugging the instrument, just as the sun was rising over the hills, the moment of his death forestalled. Such reprieve is the best for which any of us can hope.

27

When Solomon woke late that morning, it was still as a prisoner of the mountains and not as a free man. Even if Ivan Voyvoda had permitted him to depart, it would have been foolhardy to risk travelling in the mountains alone. And Ivan, who greeted him heartily when he awoke, and gave him bread and fresh goat's cheese to eat, showed every sign of wanting his guest to stay. So for a while, the mountains became Solomon's home, and the glittering dream of Constantinople—her mosques and her bazaars, her languid women and her fragrance of spices— began to fade in him.

That morning the haiduti broke camp, aiming to put as much distance as they could between themselves and the place of the raid. They headed east along the road that followed the river to Mugla, where they pitched camp for the night; and then they continued north-west to Varbovo, just across the valley from Ivan's home of Gela. Solomon found himself again in the company of strangers whose language he did not know, although Asen could serve as a translator; and as he became accustomed to the strange circumstances in which he found himself, it became apparent that the company of the haiduti was at least as congenial as that of the merchants. Perhaps he was still a prisoner, but no less so than the other men, because it matters little, in the end, whether one is a prisoner of others or a prisoner of circumstance or both: there are always constraints and bonds and chains.

Indeed, Solomon's captivity was lighter, perhaps, than that of Asen and Boyko and the others, for it soon became clear that his only duty was to play the music in the evening that brought stillness to Ivan's heart. He was excused all other labour. But then, for those few weeks, there was little labour to be had.

The period after Solomon's capture was an abundant one. The merchant convoy of which the musician had been a part had been well-laden with food; and once they were encamped at Varbovo, there was plenty to eat, and little to do other than to drink and to feast and to watch the summer clouds passing through the sky. The trees on the hills were laden with dark plums and apples, the briars heavy with blackberries, and there was trading to be done in Shiroka Luka, which was only a little distance away. So the haiduti spent their days in idleness, some of them risking secret journeys under the cover of darkness to the villages to see sweethearts and family members, others contenting themselves with exchanging stories on the hillsides, still others whittling at sticks with their knives, patching their clothes, cleaning their guns over and over, or just lying in the sun and scratching themselves. Solomon spent most of his time with his guitar, allowing the soil and the rocks and the hills and streams and the skies to teach him music different from any he had ever played before. He tried not to think of home or of the Sultan's commission. The summer was advancing fast, the air becoming colder. When the winter came, he did not know what he would do. But for now, his captivity suited him well enough. He had food to eat and time for his music; and in the evenings, when the gaidar had ceased playing his complex rhythms, Ivan Voyvoda would gesture to him, and he would take up his guitar and he would play.

The more Ivan listened to Solomon's music, the more his heart softened. Every night Ivan wept, every night he held his head in his hands and the tears flowed down in torrents; and every day, when the Voyvod rose up, the softness of the night before showed a little more in his face, the muscles less taut, the rage that had burned in his eyes ever since the day that Stoyanka had been taken a little less fierce. He spoke more often and more kindly to his men. He walked with a lighter step. When he stood against the sun, he seemed to blot out less of its light.

But the times of plenty came to an end. The stores from the raided convoy did not last forever, and shortly after the late summer rains started in earnest, Boyko came to his Voyvod and spoke with him. There is little food left, he said. The men are restless with all this idleness. They are starting to drink and to fight amongst themselves. It is time to leave this Paradise behind, as the first man and woman also left Paradise, their passage blocked by an angel with a flaming sword (at times, Boyko was prone to speaking in images and allusions: he would perhaps have made a decent priest, had life not had other plans for him). Ivan smiled at him. 'Boyko,' he said, 'my friend Boyko, let us wait a little more.'

So they waited, but Boyko was dissatisfied, and when, that night, Solomon came to play by the fire, the men grumbled and complained. Ivan silenced them with a look, Solomon took up the guitar, and the Voyvod wept.

The following day, Boyko asked again. There was a convoy headed from the south, he said. Nothing travels more quickly in the mountains than rumours, than news of strangers passing through, laden with goods. The convoy would provide rich pickings. Turks, it was said. Or city folk. One or the other. It did not really matter. The men needed food. The drink was almost gone. If they made haste, they could launch an attack at dusk, that very day.

Once more Ivan smiled and said, in the gentlest of voices, that it was not the time for battle.

Later that day, Solomon noticed a chill in the air that was not only on account of the change of the seasons. The men did not greet him as before. When he passed, they turned their backs. The guitarist found a quiet spot, shielded by rocks, and—for the first time since the night of his capture—he played the tunes he had learned in Vienna, the waltzes, the partitas, the variations on La Folia, the rondos alla Turc, the fugues, the caprices, the minuets and polonaises, the arias and ariettas, the sonatas and sonatinas. And he thought of Clara.

That evening by the fire, the men sat in surly silence. The food was less abundant than before, but there was still sufficient rakiya. The gaidar played throughout the evening, making dark sounds without joy. When he came to a halt and the Voyvod indicated that Solomon should play, the Jew felt the anger of the men, and tried to protest. 'Tonight,' he wanted to say, 'let us have no more music'; but the Voyvod made clear with a gesture that Solomon should continue. And so he did, and once he started to play the music came up from the earth and the stones and the hills and streams and the sky, and it was as if he found himself overtaken once again by the spirit of Orfei, if that was what it was—for there is in truth no way of telling—and he played so that the Voyvod wept, whilst the men looked on in mounting anger.

The day after, Boyko tried a final time. The Voyvod and his standard-bearer were standing on the hillside together, looking across the hills. 'Ivan, friend,' Boyko said, 'The convoy is still within reach. The men are hungry for action. You are our Voyvod and we are nothing without you. Please, issue the order, and we will go. I will lead the party if you wish to remain. Think of the men who love you. They cannot wait for ever.'

Ivan sighed. 'I am tired, Boyko,' he said. 'I am tired of killing. Tomorrow, perhaps. Not today.'

The atmosphere around the fire that night was heavy. The

gaidar did not play, and the men did not speak with each other. They sat in silence, drinking the remainder of the rakiya. Ivan brooded at their head, saying nothing. Asen had shot one of the captured horses earlier in the day, for food was becoming scarce and the horse was an old nag that, he judged, was better off dead than alive. They ate tough horseflesh that the fire had made bitter. When Ivan indicated Solomon should play, a ripple of anger passed through the men, but Solomon could do nothing other than obey. So once again he played, and he had never played more sweetly and strangely than on this night, a music in which the waltzes and sonatas and polonaises of his home seemed to couple with the kopanitsas and the horos and the ruchenitsas of the land in which he found himself captive, music that was incomparably sweet, but uncomfortable and strange. Ivan seemed to be listening more attentively this evening, leaning forwards and watching Solomon through the flames. He could feel the other men around the fire, circling it like an icy collar, but the flames did not draw back. And as he watched, Boyko passed the Voyvod cup upon cup of rakiya to drink.

Golyamata Mechka, the Great Bear, was lumbering overhead when Solomon put down his guitar. Ivan, the Voyvod, was sitting with closed eyes, head tilted to one side, drooling a little in his drunkenness. Solomon looked around the circle of men who were still conscious, and not one of them looked back kindly. Then Ivan collapsed sideways onto the ground, drunk, lay silent for a few moments, and let out a loud snore. Boyko looked directly at Solomon, and gestured to Asen. Asen came to stand by Boyko's side, and translated his words. Boyko spoke slowly, carefully, his eyes not leaving those of the Jew. 'Your patron,' Asen translated, 'is drunk. This being the case, it is I, Boyko, who am now in command; and I confess that I have little taste for music.' Then Boyko took out his pistol and pointed it at the musician. Several of the men got to their feet. 'Come with me,'

Boyko said. Asen rendered his words into German. 'Bring your guitar.'

28

Ivan Voyvoda woke before dawn. The fire had burned down to faintly glowing embers, the other men were gone, and the morning star hung in a sky that was slowly turning pale in the East. In a nearby tree, a few birds sang. Ivan scrambled over the low rise and looked across the valley. Shiroka Luka slept below, and further to the south, he could see the rounded hills of his home village, Gela. If he had spent the summers since his departure from home in these mountains, he had never returned to his natal village. The pain of it would be too terrible to bear; but now that he looked at it in the pre-dawn light, he found once again that tears were beginning to gather at the corners of his eyes. He wiped them away with his sleeve and then stood to make a tour of the encampment. The men were all asleep in their tents. He could hear them snoring. He thought of the coming winter, the long journey to Skopje, the months in the monastery; and he wondered how he would survive those cold months. Bogdan had befriended a fox, he remembered. The fox had sustained him through the cold months. He smiled to remember Bogdan, who had been kind to him in his distress, who had knocked him to the ground and then given him food to eat, who had died at the place called Haidushki Dol. Bogdan had a fox that padded on delicate feet to the window of his monastery cell to be fed scraps; but Ivan had no need of foxes: he wanted only music.

It was then that he noticed that Solomon's tent was left

open. He walked over and put his bearded head through the door. The man and his guitar were gone. Ivan started to shake with a terrible anger. The bastard, he said to himself. The bastard has fled. He has taken his guitar and fled down to Shiroka Luka. From there he has taken the road east. He has fled to work for the Sultan, to play his music for the scrofulous Mahmud who sits upon his throne in Constantinople and brings down misery after misery upon his people. As this thought took shape, Ivan felt the return of the anger that, for the last few weeks, had been held at bay by Solomon's music. He welcomed the fury back into the chambers of his heart, feeling the way it flooded his breast with life, the way it made his blood pulse faster in his veins. The bastard has absconded, and if he has not put enough distance behind him on his traitorous flight, he will understand that the hospitality of Ivan Voyvoda is not something to be refused lightly.

The morning star burned. Ivan pulled his pistol from his belt, took a rifle from his tent and headed down the track that led from the encampment to Shiroka Luka, calling down such curses upon poor Solomon that even the earth might have trembled to hear them. He turned off the path and walked east along the ridge that overlooked the village. He had been walking for no more than a half hour when saw the cross, silhouetted against the morning sky some fifty yards from the track, as if in the night some pilgrim had hewn the trunks of trees, bound them together and set them up as a sign of devotion to Our Lord. Ivan hesitated. He turned from the track and waded through the long grass and brambles to the foot of the cross. A dark shape hung from the wood, not quite the shape of a man. Ivan squinted, to see better in the clear morning light. There, nailed to the wood, was Solomon Kuretic, the guitarist who had once been the toast of Vienna, who had played music sweet enough to ease the sufferings of Ivan's heart. He was not breathing. Ivan could see the dark smudge on his breast where his killers, whether in a final moment of mercy, or whether out of a need to make sure that the man was actually dead, had put a bullet in his chest. Round his neck, on a piece of rope, was hung the guitar, its face broken. Ivan reached up towards the figure, feeling his side. The body was cold. He then looked down, and in the pale light he could see the white pages of a book, inscribed in square letters, torn and scattered around through the brambles and the weeds.

Ivan Voyvoda, a man feared everywhere from the Danube to Constantinople, whose name was known and respected even in the palace of Mahmud II, knelt at the foot of the cross and embraced the rough wood; and, in the place that to this day is still known simply as Solomon, his body was shaken by wave upon wave of grief.

29

Red light was still trickling over the dark pines in the east and down in the valley the river seemed to burn. Torn wisps of cloud fringed the rising sun like bloody standards. Ivan hugged the foot of the cross, weeping as Saint John or the Mother of God wept in the golden icons that gleamed out of the darkness of incense-heavy churches. But there were no priests to intone the liturgy, only the morning insects that chirruped with the coming sun, only the birds—a busy flight of goldfinches, a kite circling overhead for early prey. On the cross, Solomon's body hung lifeless. In the dawn light, it was possible to see something like a shadow in the brambles and the damp grass, the place where the wood had been laid whilst the haiduti hammered nails through Solomon's hands and feet. To the south and north—for the cross had been erected to face the east—were dark traces of blood. Then there was a strange sound, sharply metallic, followed by a buzz, a low thrum, a flurry of lingering overtones. The bottom string of the guitar, the lower E, had snapped. Ivan half rose to his feet, put his shoulder to the wood and started to push.

At first the cross did not budge. It remained where it had been planted in the earth. Then the wood creaked and Ivan let out a groan. A fissure appeared in the recently-trampled earth, the cross wavered a little, and the guitar knocked against the wood, its broken body echoing with sound from the remaining five strings. Ivan pushed harder, the earth by his feet erupted and the cross seemed to hesitate before it tilted and, with a grating sound, fell back into the undergrowth. Ivan stepped forward and looked into Solomon's face. His eyes were still open, as was his mouth. The dead, they say, are at peace; but Ivan had seen many corpses, and had not seen peace in a single one of them. With his right hand, he closed the Jew's eyes. Then he lifted the guitar from around his neck and placed it gently on the ground. A deep fracture ran through the cedar wood of the guitar's face, but the rest of the body was unharmed. The broken string hung loosely, stained with the grease of Solomon's hands.

Solomon's hands: they were dark with blood and torn by the nails that had been driven through them: one in the left and two in the right. Ivan touched the cold fingers. Then he turned away from the body. He took the rope that had been used to suspend the guitar around the musician's neck and he tied the guitar to his own back. The sun was fully risen now, the crickets becoming louder. Ivan turned his back to the sun and headed west, making for the encampment.

That summer, the river that flowed through the valley of Shiroka Luka was filled with an abundance of mottled trout, hanging suspended in the water in the shadow of the bank overhung with coiled ferns. The air was thick with the woven blue and green traces of dragonflies. And on that same morning that Ivan found Solomon crucified, not far away across the dark pines and the forests of beech and oak, in the village of Gela, the woman who had given birth to Ivan woke from her bed and thought of her son, as she did every morning at dawn, and at noon and at dusk. She woke to the sound of the cocks crowing thrice, crowing four times, crowing endlessly; and she thought of her son and knew that he was near. She called to her husband and said, 'Husband! I dreamed of our son!' And her husband replied: 'Yes, I too have dreamed.'

And then they fell silent, for there was nothing else to be said.

30

Boyko, Asen and all the others were still sleeping when Ivan returned to the camp. It had been a long night: it is hard work to take a man, drag him weeping and pleading through the countryside, and to nail his body to a roughly hewn cross; and so the haiduti were sleeping the satisfied, undisturbed sleep of those who have discharged all of their duties and obligations, lost in the separate worlds of their various dreams. Ivan went to Solomon's tent first of all, and gathered up the musician's small bag. He rummaged through, but there was very little of interest; only a letter, written in the Latin script. He took the letter and tucked it inside his tunic. Then he left Solomon's tent and went to the tent of the gaidar, for no other reason than he was a musician, as Solomon had been a musician, and revenge is a desire that is born out of a love of symmetry. The player was just stirring, and had himself played no part in the events of the night before, but Ivan was ignorant of the man's innocence, and as the man tried to rise up, Ivan took his pistol from his belt and pulled the trigger. The man's mouth gaped open, his eyes spoke puzzlement for a moment, then he collapsed backwards.

Ivan emerged from the tent. At the sound of the gunshot, the camp was in uproar. The haiduti scrambled with rifles and pistols and knives, hitching up their trousers and coming out into the light. They expected a party of Ottoman troops, but instead they saw Ivan, standing outside the gaidar's tent,

Solomon's broken guitar on his back. The men emerged one by one, and then fell silent. Ivan looked at their puzzled faces—his brothers, his followers—and roared a challenge. 'I have killed the gaidar,' he said, 'and I will kill you all. Who is next?'

None of the men moved.

'Who killed the Jew?' he bellowed. 'Tell me, you bastards, which one of you it was who killed the Jew?'

Ivan's men did not reply. They were standing at various distances, and each one of them had a gun raised. Any one of them could have pulled the trigger and sent Ivan to the next world in a moment, but he was their Voyvod, and this was enough to still their hands.

'Tell me who killed the Jew. Asen? Boyko? Vasily?' He ran through their names one by one. None of the men replied.

Then Boyko stepped forward. 'It was for you that he was killed,' he said.

Ivan started to shudder, the gun in his hand shaking. He let it fall to the ground. 'Which one of you is man enough to fight me unarmed? Come, Boyko, if you wish to challenge me, then let us put our weapons away and let us fight, as honourable men.'

Boyko smiled sadly. 'I have no desire to fight you, nor to challenge you, my Voyvod. I only wish to restore you to what you were before.'

'How would you have me restored?'

Boyko kept his gun trained upon Ivan. 'You have become as pliant as a girl in love,' he said. 'The Jew's music has made you soft. We have little food remaining, we must go raiding again before the season is finished, and yet you have spent your days sitting here and dreaming.' He was going to add, 'like a woman,' for Boyko, who could have made a good priest if life had not decided otherwise on his behalf, had no love of women. But he suppressed the impulse. Ivan was his Voyvod.

The Voyvod did not respond. He looked at the faces of his men. The men kept their pistols trained on him.

'We want you back, Ivan of Gela,' Boyko said. 'The musician was enchanting you. He was casting a spell over you. It was witchcraft, the way that he made you soft. We killed him not out of hatred, but out of our love for you. We killed him out of the friendship we bear towards you.'

'Who held the hammer?' asked Ivan.

Asen inclined his head.

Ivan took a second pistol from his belt and pointed it at Asen. Asen lowered his own pistol. 'Ivan,' he whispered. But the Voyvod looked him in the eye, exactly in the way that he had done many times by the fire when raising their glasses and toasting each other, and he pulled the trigger. Asen fell down dead.

Ivan looked back at Boyko. 'Who raised the cross?' he asked.

Two more men shifted their position. Ivan shot first one and then the other. Neither man attempted to return fire. Ivan smiled. 'Ah,' he said, 'so you are all still loyal?'

'We are still loyal,' Boyko replied. 'You are our Voyvod. We wish only one thing, that you forgive us for killing the Jew who worked witchcraft over you. We have killed better men, all of us. Do not hold this thing against us.'

'And if I do not forgive you?' Ivan asked.

Boyko looked around at the other men, those who were still standing. 'Then,' he said, 'we can no longer follow you.'

Ivan shifted his weight and looked down at the ground. The sun was no longer red. The air tasted of autumn.

'Boyko,' said Ivan, 'how little you understand. Only Solomon the Jew had the power to ease my suffering heart. And now he is gone.'

'Our suffering is our strength,' Boyko said grimly.

Ivan looked at him for a few seconds, and then he turned

his pistol round in his hand, so the handle was pointing outwards and the barrel was pointing directly at his own stomach. 'Then I pray that one day the Lord may make us weak,' he said. 'Come, Boyko, take my gun. I am leaving.'

Boyko hesitated.

'Boyko Voyvoda, come. I no longer wish for this life. Come. Take my gun. Kill me if you like, for I have slaughtered four of your best men. Take my gun, Boyko Voyvoda. Ivan is Voyvoda no longer.'

Boyko put his own gun down and walked the twenty paces to where Ivan stood. He curled his fingers around the handle of the gun. Ivan let go of the barrel, so that had Boyko wanted, he could have pulled the trigger and put the former Voyvod out of his misery. And perhaps that is what Ivan wanted; but if it was, he was disappointed. Boyko had too much love in him, or too much bitterness, to oblige. The new Voyvod lowered the gun and the two men gazed into each other's eyes.

'You will need a standard-bearer, Boyko,' Ivan said, breaking Boyko's gaze. 'I was fortunate to have a standard-bearer such as you. May you be as fortunate as I was.' He turned away. 'Now let me leave.'

Boyko did not say a word. Ivan scratched at his beard, looked around the men. He took his rifle from his back where it was slung along with the guitar. Unarmed, save for the knife that he still carried inside his clothing, he looked somehow more fierce than he had armed. 'Do what you will with my rifle,' he said. 'I have no further use for it.'

Then, without saying another word, he left, shambling through the early morning mist, heading along the road that led north, away from the mountains that had been his home, Solomon's guitar slung over his shoulder, the letter snug inside his tunic.

Part Three

The Musician

31

The night after Solomon's death, Boyko and those of his men who remained sat around the fire, looking into the flames. The haiduti had spent the afternoon burying their fallen comrades. The dead lay in the earth with their mouths open in surprise, not yet accustomed to finding themselves underground. Boyko held Ivan's gun in his hand, feeling its weight. Up above, he could trace the constellations his mother had described to him when he was still a child. Since Ivan's departure, few of the men had spoken. They had performed the funeral rites wordlessly, then had built a fire and seated themselves. The music was finished, the gaidar deep beneath the soil, his pipes laid by his side. The men drank rakiya in silence.

Some distance off, to the north, was another fire. Ivan had walked northwards on remote paths through the mountains and the meadows, filled with rage and with the terror of rage; and he had continued walking into the night, until fatigue overcame him. When he squatted down and built his fire, he thought briefly of his fellow haiduti. He had never been a man who loved the conversation of others, who relished dancing the horo and raising glasses with his companions; and yet that night, as he sat with the guitar in his lap, the guitar that had belonged to Solomon who hung dead upon the cross on the hillside near Shiroka Luka, he felt a terrible loneliness sweep through his body, a physical loneliness that seemed to seep up from the ground through his feet to wrap itself around his heart. He reached into his tunic for the letter that he had taken from Solomon's bag, and squinted at the text, but could not comprehend it. He folded it and returned it to his tunic.

The night was a beautiful one. Stars fell from the skies in their multitudes. In the woods, a long way off, the wolves were howling, but they would not trouble him. Night birds coughed and stirred. Ivan was not insensible to the beauty, but the brutality of the years that he had endured, and that had come to an end that very day had taken its toll. His heart was like a ruined mansion that was now the abode of wild beasts, the walls wound about with ivy. The rain came straight through the roof. The beauty of the hillside, the scent of the night flowers, the stars that tumbled from the heavens, as brief as lives, the crackle and spit of the fire—these things were hard for Ivan to endure. Ivan sat with the guitar in his lap. And then—perhaps it was at the instigation of the spirit of his uncle who, long before, had hanged himself in a rain of yellow cherry blossom; or it was on account of the obscure prompting of Solomon from beyond the grave, if beyond the grave there is not only earth, and beyond the earth more earth still; or it was at the urging of the old dismembered king Orfei, whose blood had soaked into that soil, calling to Ivan across the centuries—as he cradled the guitar on his lap, the thumb of his right hand started to caress the five good strings, whilst the fingers of his left hand bunched uneasily upon the finger-board.

The sound, at first, was not beautiful, but the guitar is a generous instrument: it does not screech and protest at the touch of a beginner as does a violin. So Ivan played more gently, his breath hanging on the night air that, in spite of the fire, was becoming cold. And, for all the rough clumsiness of his fingers, despite the broken bass string and the guitar's fractured sound-board, as he stroked the guitar a tune started to emerge, a succession of notes on the A and D strings, a melody that was unadorned at first, but that he then repeated, embellishing it with stumbling ornaments and grace-notes. He broke off, and tried the melody a second time, but this time up on the higher strings, further up the finger-board; the same melody, but first an octave, then two octaves, above. The guitar sang in a voice like a woman's, like the way women sing when they think that they are alone, when they have nobody to sing to except themselves. As the tune became more confident, less stumbling, Ivan looked down in astonishment at those hands that were used to being balled into fists for fighting, scarcely comprehending that those fingers accustomed to strangling or to grasping knives and rifles could be the source of such beauty, and he closed his eyes and let them do what they would, because who knows where music comes from?

With the music came the stilling of the rage that he had endured that morning, the rage that had gripped him ever since Stoyanka's abduction. But this stillness was too painful to endure for long. He placed the guitar by his side and looked into the flames until they died down and the pallid dawn spread over the hillside. When the sun had fully risen, without having slept, Ivan rose to his feet, slung the guitar over his back and, without looking back—because as Orfei found to his cost, if you do not want to lose forever that which you love, you must resist the temptation to look back—he headed north once again, making for the Danube.

Somewhere towards the south, Boyko was sitting by the dying embers of the fire. He, too, had not slept for the entire night, and with the dawn at last the depth of his weariness became apparent to him. He put Ivan's gun in his belt, nodded to those of his companions who were still awake, and walked down the hill towards the stream. He followed the stream until it met with the river, and there he crossed by means of a low bridge. Half way across, he stopped, leaning on the balustrade. He let the gun fall into the tumbling waters below. There was a splash and it was gone. He leaned there for some time. A dipper came, fat and busy, hopping and fluttering from rock to rock, looking for insects. Boyko felt the sun on his face. The bird departed, and Boyko turned down the track that would lead him back home, to the village of his birth.

32

With the sun at his back, that same morning Ivan started on the long walk that took him over the Balkan mountains to the plains, and from there to the shores of the river. He was making for Vienna, where Solomon the Jew had lived. He did not know why, nor what he would find there, and his imagination faltered before the thought of the famous city that he had heard of only in stories; but he had in his possession the letter he could not understand, and he had in his ears the memory of the Jew's music, and he had at his back a morass of suffering. These three things were enough to navigate by.

For food and shelter, he relied upon the kindness of strangers. As long as he kept away from the large towns and the cities, where the people were immersed in indifference, and as long as he lodged with simple people who lived with their feet planted in the soil, there was kindness enough. Some nights he had to spend beneath the sky with only his guitar for company. At these times, when he was alone, he played, coaxing tunes out of the guitar and out of the depths of his memory. When the rage began to rise in him, he only had to pick up the guitar and pluck a tune, or even just stroke a single string and listen to its thrumming slowly attenuate and die away, and he would find calm again; but when he was not playing, the rage was always lying in wait, ready to return at the slightest provocation. This was the other reason that he avoided the cities and was careful not to spend too much time in the company of others. What he feared, above all else, was his own self, the fury that had been planted in his heart on the night that Stoyanka was taken from him, that he had nurtured every winter in the monastery outside Skopje, that had been fed by the blood of those he had killed. He wanted no more of it, and although the guitar could soften the fury, he knew that he was not free of it; so he was circumspect, shunning the company of those who might provoke him.

Only once during his journey to Vienna did the rage get the better of him, when he was set upon by two men on a remote track, and it was only when he had knocked one to the ground and put his knife to the throat of the other that he realised what he was doing. He swallowed the rage, sheathing his knife, and fled from the two men. The rest of that night he spent shivering on the hillside with a strange fear: not the fear of death or of pain, for he was accustomed to this; but the fear of all he was capable of doing.

He could have followed the Danube westwards were it not for the fact that all along the river there were towns and cities, so he made his way across country, walking with a kind of stoic determination, and when he found himself without lodgings he made use of haylofts and barns as the autumn turned to early winter. He entered Vienna on Christmas Day of 1822, when the bells were ringing in the churches and the people of the city were preparing for the feast. He took the letter from his tunic and showed it to passers-by, and they pointed him the way until he came to the house of Karl Toepfer. By the time he arrived he was fatigued and cold; and when Toepfer opened the door, Ivan fell to his knees and thrust the letter towards him.

Toepfer, who was both a guitarist and a philosopher, responded in the most phlegmatic fashion imaginable at the unexpected arrival of a fierce-looking foreigner in clothes soiled by days upon the road, who appeared kneeling by his front door on the feast of Christ's birth, burbling in a barbaric tongue that Toepfer did not understand, holding before him the broken guitar that had once belonged—Toepfer never forgot a guitar— to his pupil Solomon Kuretic. Toepfer invited him in. He was not a man who could, on the Feast of Our Lord, allow another man to freeze in the winter cold of Vienna whilst he and his family were feasting.

The musician's wife, a capable and somewhat large woman who was a long-time adherent of the religion of common sense, and who stood upon the face of the earth with such formidable self-assurance that few ever dared to cross her, ushered him to the table to join the feast. She fetched a plate and a knife and sawed slabs of meat for the guest, then she cut a large slice of bread to accompany the meat and handed the plate to Ivan. The couple's two children, who were already seated at the table, gazed upon the stranger with awe—a girl and a boy, aged six and eight. They giggled at this strange man as he fell upon the food, using his hands to tear apart the meat, stuffing great fistfuls of food, running with grease, into his mouth. Meanwhile, Toepfer read through the letter.

The text was laconic. Kuretic told of his capture by bandits. He said that he was being well treated, but that he did not know if he would be in Constantinople by the winter. He asked Toepfer to send his warmest wishes to Clara, and to tell her not to worry. He said that he had his guitar for consolation. It served this purpose well, he said. In the evenings he played, and the playing was a balm for the homesickness. If he was fortunate enough to return to Vienna some time in the future, he concluded, then he would have learned much in the ways of music from his sojourn in the land of Orpheus, where his life had been saved by the music that he played, and by the kindness of a man called Ivan.

Toepfer folded the letter up again and placed it in his breast pocket. He glanced at his wife. 'It is from Solomon,' he said.

'He was captured.' Frau Toepfer breathed in sharply, then continued to serve the family. They ate in silence, until the unexpected visitor was wiping his red lips with his sleeves. Frau Toepfer dismissed the children, who left with reluctance, creeping away from the table and, the moment they were out of the door, tumbling and giggling along the hall.

'My friend,' her husband said. 'Tell me your name.'

Ivan did not respond, so Toepfer pointed to his own chest. 'Karl Toepfer,' he said. 'I am Karl Toepfer.'

Ivan seemed to understand. 'Ivàn,' he said, with the same cadence that his mother had spoken his name, whilst he had still been sleeping in her womb. 'Ivàn Gelski.'

Toepfer smiled. 'Welcome, Ivan Gelski,' he said. 'Welcome. Tell me, are you a guitarist?' He mimed if he was playing the guitar.

Ivan inclined his head. 'Kitara,' he said.

'You play kitara?'

Ivan looked bewildered, so Toepfer picked up Solomon's guitar and examined it closely. It was damaged, but not irreparably so. He started to unwind the broken string, which he pulled away so that only the five good strings remained. 'Solomon,' he said. 'This is the guitar of my friend Solomon. He says in his letter that he knew you. Can you play it for me?'

At the mention of Solomon's name, Ivan looked directly at Toepfer. He did not have the words to say what he wished to say, so instead he put out his hand and repeated the word 'Kitara' but this time with the upward inflection of a question. Toepfer passed him the guitar. Ivan put it in his lap and started to play. It was the same tune that he had played on the hillside north of Shiroka Luka on the first night of his exile. His playing was rough, without technique. But the moment he played the first note—a single note is all it takes—Toepfer knew not only that Solomon was dead, but that the man who sat before him was a musician of uncommon talent. Toepfer's wife, herself an accomplished player on the guitar, hunched her shoulders and nodded her head. Toepfer thought of Solomon, and his eyes started to fill with tears.

When Ivan came to a close, the husband and wife sat back in silence, listening to the final notes on the open bass strings fading into nothing. The winter dark was gathering outside, and the fire was crackling in the grate. The musician looked up at Toepfer and his wife, and then he spread his hands wide and lowered his head, a strangely courtly gesture.

'You must stay with us,' said Toepfer quietly. 'You have talent. I can train you. My wife can teach you the German tongue. She is a good teacher. And one day we will be able to talk, and you will be able to tell me what became of Solomon.'

Ivan looked at him without understanding, but the rhythm of the language lulled him. He understood he was safe. There by the fire, he had the curious sensation of a life surrounded by gentleness and kindness, and the sensation was so novel to him, so unexpected, that he did not know what to do with it.

Outside, the first snow of the year was beginning to fall.

33

Ivan remained in Vienna for more than three years. By the time
he left, Karl Toepfer had trained him in everything he knew of
the artistry of the guitar, yet the Bulgar's technique remained
eccentric. In the early days, during the long mornings Toepfer
taught Ivan's hands how to caress the finger-board of the guitar
that had once belonged to Solomon, now restored, restrung and,
most curiously of all, richer in sound on account of its misfortune
endured in the Rhodope mountains. Toepfer taught Ivan's body
how to embrace the guitar, how to bring lightness to the playing
of arpeggios, and how to make scale passages run like the trickling
of water. He taught him how to angle his arm and his hand,
and how to coax a sweetness out of the guitar by bringing his
right hand close to the sound-hole, and how to play with a
metallic sharpness with his hand by the bridge.

Ivan played from the very beginning in the style of Aguado,
using his fingernails. It was unorthodox, and yet there was
something in this that was, Toepfer recognised, essential to the
sound. For even when he played the most simple of studies,
those by Carulli and Carcassi, there was something about Ivan's
technique that seemed to come from far off, from beyond the
mountains, a spirit bred in a wholly other place. A worse teacher
than Toepfer would have attempted to have exorcised this spirit
from out of him, to have clipped his nails and to have driven it
away; but from the moment he first heard it, Toepfer recognised
that this was one of those manifestations of that deep pulse that

lay at the heart of things, the spirit that causes us to live and to go on living, despite everything: and so he nourished it.

As Ivan came to understand the art of the guitar, he learned how music had the power to still his own passions, as Solomon's music had once stilled him. Yet he came to see with increasing clarity that this stillness was only temporary. On occasion, when he was away from his guitar, when he least expected it, his heart would lie in snarling ambush for him. At these times, he dreaded that the rage and bitterness that Bogdan had promised might altogether overwhelm him, and he fled back to his guitar to pluck at the strings until his heart was silent once again, until the rage and bitterness had passed.

In the afternoons, Toepfer's wife taught Ivan German. She was a patient and determined teacher, but the Bulgar never took to reading and writing. A man should talk face-to-face, he believed, or else he should be silent. All else was worthless and just added to the noise of the world. Nevertheless, he had a quick mind and learned easily. Within a year, he could converse without too much difficulty; and as his fluency grew, so Toepfer drew out of him the story of Solomon, and the story that had led to this story, and many other stories besides, because once one has started to follow the thread of a single story, one is led further and further away from home, out into this world that extends in all directions without any ending. It developed into a trade of sorts: every day Toepfer gave Ivan all he knew of music, and in return Ivan spoke of Solomon, of the hills and the streams and the upland meadows. It took more than two years before Toepfer had a clear idea of how Solomon had died. Once he knew, his philosopher's sense of duty—he had read most of Kant, and agreed with some of it—impelled him to pay a visit to his cousin Clara one evening, so that he might speak with her in confidence.

When she had first heard the news of Solomon's death, not

that long after Ivan's arrival in Vienna, Clara had shed a few tears: not so much tears born out of a new sadness as tears provoked by the recollection of a sadness already endured, for when Solomon departed from Vienna, she had already given up hope of ever seeing him again. For Clara there was no great difference between leaving Vienna and leaving the earth, there was only the finest of lines between a departure for the city of Constantinople and for the City of the Dead. As a result, by the time that the news of Solomon's death reached her, she had already gone through the full course of mourning; and now, almost three years after she had last set eyes upon her former lover, she was little inclined to speak with her cousin about a matter that she thought already long settled. Nevertheless, she greeted Toepfer warmly, inviting him in to drink coffee, but she seemed distracted, or perhaps a little bored, at the mention of Solomon's name. Over coffee, Toepfer clasped her by the hands and gazed at her with such imploring determination that she at last consented to hear him out. Toepfer was a man of considerable tact. He did not tell her of Ivan's part in Solomon's abduction, speaking only of the Bulgar as a man of the mountains, a man who had befriended Solomon and whom Solomon had taught to love music. 'Herr Gelski is a strange man,' he said to his cousin, 'but it might ease your suffering to know that Solomon's music is reborn in his.'

Clara sighed. 'Do not talk of Solomon,' she whispered. 'And do not come here to tell me of Herr Gelski's talents. Again and again you tell the whole of Vienna this, but not once has Herr Gelski performed on the stage. You are making a fool of yourself, Karl.'

Toepfer looked awkward. 'Herr Gelski plays like none other, it is true,' he said. 'And if he has no desire to take to the concert stage, then I will not attempt to persuade him. I am sure, however, that if I asked him, he would play for you. Just for you, Clara.'

A look of displeasure passed over Clara's face, tightening her lips. 'Karl, you are too kind to this man who stays in your house and who eats your food. Your wife has taught him to speak the German language, you claim to have taught him almost all you know of the guitar, and yet this kindness is useless if Herr Gelski's talents remain hidden.'

But Karl just smiled. 'It is not a kindness. It is a privilege,' he said, 'to have a pupil who outstrips oneself in skill and in talent. There is no greater privilege than this.'

Clara did not smile back. 'Karl,' she said, 'you are too much a philosopher.'

Over the months that followed, however, it became clear that the trade that had sustained both Toepfer and Ivan was coming to an end. Toepfer had no more to teach Ivan; and Ivan had no more stories to tell. His homeland had become increasingly distant to him, and as he walked through the streets of Vienna, he felt as if he belonged nowhere, neither in that city on the Danube, nor back towards the land of his birth. To return would be to surround himself with the reminders of his suffering—the hills and the streams and the village girls with their posies and the lament of the gaida that sounds like a lost sheep strayed far from the fold; and surrounded by such residue, how easily he might be overcome by the bitterness coiled in his heart.

One evening in the autumn, Ivan was walking by the Danube with Toepfer. They had spent most of their walk in silence, and at a certain point they came to a halt. The sun was turning the river a spectacular colour of gold. Toepfer looked round at his pupil. 'You seem restless, Herr Gelski.'

Ivan did not respond. He looked out over the river. There was a boat, some way out, and he could hear people laughing and joking. 'This river flows to my homeland,' said Ivan. His now fluent German was thick and rolling. He paused. 'What you say is true: I am restless.'

'You have outdone me, Ivan. There is no more that I can teach you.'

Dark against the golden skeins of cloud: a flight of geese in formation. The boat was drifting downstream. The voices faded to nothing as the boat headed into the distance. 'And yet,' said Ivan, 'I still have more to learn.'

Toepfer turned to face him. 'Yours is a rare talent,' he said. 'You have gone further than any other. If there is anyone who can still teach you, you must leave Vienna. I know of only one more skilled than you: the Spaniard, Ferdinand Sor.'

'Sor?' he asked. The name was familiar to him. In the early days he had played some of the Spaniard's studies. 'Is he not in Moscow?'

'He is recently returned to Paris. In the past he and I have exchanged correspondence. If you still have the desire to learn, then I recommend that you go to Paris and apprentice yourself to the Spaniard. I could write you a letter of introduction.'

Ivan closed his eyes. He could hear the geese, a long way off. Then he opened his eyes again. 'I would be grateful,' he said. 'I would be very grateful.'

34

The sickness was getting worse, and the rain did not help. It made him long for the clear cold of Moscow. Or for the warm sun of Spain. But not London, that wretched town with her mist and her foul odours that drifted up from the all but lifeless river, and her squat, charmless citizens. He longed for everywhere except London.

Ferdinand pulled the blankets more closely around himself, and leaned towards the fire. The rain was streaming down the window with steady determination, as if it did not intend to let up for weeks. Through the glass, he could see low clouds, brown and heavy. He shivered again, and muttered a prayer to the Virgin in Spanish, the prayer that as a boy he had intoned every morning in the monastery school of Montserrat, and that was almost the only thing that remained of what had once been his faith. These days, he only used Spanish for prayers and curses, an exile not only from his homeland but also from his own tongue; and the memory of that monastery between those strange rocks, where you could smell the sea on the air, and where the hillsides were filled with the sounds of the practising choirs, was one that made the cold seem even more severe. He sneezed and looked gloomily into the flames.

This sickness had happened before, and he knew it was not serious. He had learned to endure much worse cold during those crystalline winters in Moscow when Félicité, wrapped in furs, her cheeks red as apples, would put her small gloved hand in his, and they would walk through the streets nodding to acquaintances and admirers. She had been the brazier at which he had warmed himself for those years in Russia, and despite her small frame, he had believed then that her body could provide fuel and warmth enough for the remainder of his life, were it not for the others who, his jealous eye had already long noted, clamoured to steal a bit of that same warmth for themselves.

He had endured much worse, and yet this late autumn damp, without Félicité to make him warm broth and to put her arms around him and to reassure him that the sickness would not last, was insufferable. Their journey back from Moscow had been frigid, despite the clear and generous sunshine that is peculiar to September and that had blessed them for every mile of the way. It had been so different from the journey they had taken together from London to Moscow three years before, cuddling in the back of the coach, giggling in lodging houses, when he had been astonished at her youth and her beauty and the suppleness of her body.

He heard a knock at the door. It opened before he could say anything. He hoped it might be Félicité, for he had not seen her for several days; but instead it was Antoine Meissonnier, dressed immaculately, an urbane smile that was impossible to read on his face, and a sheaf of papers underneath his arms. The sufferer sneezed again.

'Ferdinand,' said the visitor. 'You are still sick?'

Ferdinand sneezed again by way of assent.

'I trust that Félicité looks after you well.' There was a kind of flicker in his smile that made Ferdinand uneasy.

'Very well, thank you,' he said.

'She is acclimatising to Paris again, after so long away?'

'I believe so. Antoine, please, sit down.' Ferdinand indicated to a chair.

Antoine arranged himself in the chair carefully, crossing his long legs. 'I have brought the proofs,' he smiled. 'Would you care to take a look?'

Ferdinand reached out from underneath the blanket and took the papers. He looked through, nodding as he did so.

'Of course, you will want to examine them more carefully when you are not so inconvenienced by illness, but you should find everything is in order. It is, if you do not mind me saying, a fine collection. A first-class collection. I am particularly moved by the Opus 28. It was written, I presume, in Moscow?'

'Torzhok,' the other man said. 'We spent several days in Torzhok. They embroider the most beautiful figures out of gold. I bought a dress for Félicité to wear. We walked along the river in the sunshine under the willow trees...' The memory seemed to precipitate him into a fresh bout of melancholy and he shuddered pathetically, his teeth chattering together. 'Antoine,' he said after a few moments, regaining a sense of his composure, 'may I offer you brandy?'

'No, thank you,' Antoine smiled. 'It is still early.'

'You do not mind if I do?'

'By all means.'

He placed the papers down on a table, slipped off the cocoon of blankets and got to his feet. Antoine suspected that he was afflicted more by sadness than by the cold that was causing him to sneeze, and as he watched the sick man pour himself a brandy, he wondered at the precise reason for this gloomy humour. Ferdinand drank the brandy standing up, then he returned to his chair by the fire and enshrouded himself once again in the blankets. Antoine looked out of the window. The rain was easing a little. 'I should be departing,' he said. 'I only wished to bring you the proofs for your approval. It is, as I have already said, magnificent work.' He smiled with his teeth but not with his eyes.

Ferdinand propped his head on his hand. He could feel the hot brandy as it burned somewhere half way down his throat.

'You are performing tonight?' Antoine asked.

Ferdinand nodded. 'Will you be there?'

Antoine looked apologetic. 'I am a busy man, Ferdinand. I have an appointment to keep, so I will not be present. But I wish you well. I hope that the performance is a success.' He got to his feet. 'I should depart,' he said. 'Goodbye.'

Ferdinand opened his eyes and looked up. 'Goodbye,' he said.

When Antoine had left, Ferdinand coughed for a while, as if he wished to remind himself that he was still ill, and then he pulled the papers towards him and placed them on his lap. He started to leaf through the pages. Opus numbers twenty-four to twenty-nine. He turned to number twenty-eight and looked through the music. Antoine was right: it was magnificent. He started to hum, following the lines of the staves with his eyes.

35

36

Malbrough s'en va-t-en guerre,
  mironton, mironton, mirontaine,
  Malbrough s'en va-t-en guerre,
  on n' sait quand il reviendra.
Il reviendra-z-à Pâques,
  mironton, mironton, mirontaine,
  Il reviendra-z-à Pâques,
  ou à la Trinité.
La Trinité se passe,
  mironton, mironton, mirontaine,
  la Trinité se passe,
  Malbrough ne revient pas.

It is said that when Goethe travelled the roads of Europe in the late eighteenth century, he nursed in his breast a growing hatred for the Duke of Marlborough. This was not on account of any personal slight, for Goethe had never met the Duke nor did he know anything of him. The reason was solely that of the song that took the Duke's name, or something very like it: the Malbroug Air. This was a song that had been sung to the dauphin in his nursery, that was known in the homes of the rich and was a lullaby at the cradles of the poor, that was favoured even by Napoleon who, as he went about his business, was known to hum it quietly to himself. As he travelled here and there, the wretched tune rang in the great German writer's ears; it reappeared again and again at every music evening he attended; whether in the cities or in small taverns, it tormented him, this tune that was later to become mixed up in stories about bears and mountains and the coming and going of the former, to see what they could see, this tune that was born somewhere in the Arab world and was carried to Europe by crusaders and merchants, this tune that has outlived all of those who have passed it on from mouth to mouth, reborn again and again like the soul as dreamed of by Plato, always the same soul, always different. And thus by a kind of metempsychosis, this curious tune that had about it more of the characteristics of God than of men—seemingly immortal where men are mortal; apparently omnipresent where men can only be in one place at once— eventually reappeared in Ferdinand Sor's Opus 28, *Introduction et Variations sur l'Air Marlbroug.* Yet whether because of the natural sadness of the Muscovite climate, because of the black gloom that was an ineradicable part of the composer's soul, or because the tune itself, after such long travelling, was becoming tired and homesick, by the time it was reprised by Ferdinand's pen, what was usually taken to be a light and trivial melody, fit for the nursery of a dauphin and the idle moments of an Emperor, it had become dark and brooding, a melody that, for all of the artfulness of its construction, was almost entirely without light.

The composer sat by the fireside, nursing his cold and his unhappy heart, turning the pages of the proofs and humming through the variations. Outside the window the rain continued to come down in sheets. Somewhere not far away the composer's publisher, the estimable Antoine Meissonnier of the Boulevard de Montmartre, went hurrying through the streets on his way home. And Ferdinand himself was also a traveller over seas and mountains: Ferdinand Sors, Fernando Sor, Ferdinando Sor, Ferran Sors—he was a man with many names, a man who moved from one name to another with a restless nomadism, known in this city in this fashion, and in another city in another, such that he sometimes thought himself to be a series of variations upon a theme that was already forgotten.

As the afternoon wore on, the sick man (let us not call him a malingerer, for not knowing the condition of his soul, we would be unwise to sit in judgement upon him) tired at last of sitting by the fire which had begun to burn down in the grate; and so he got to his feet and, taking the sheaf of papers left by Meissonnier, he walked to the next-door room, where his guitar lay upon a couch. He picked up the instrument and slumped into the seat, swinging his feet up, so that the guitar was laid across his belly. With the flesh of the thumb of his right hand, he stroked the strings. He deplored the barbarism of Aguado, convinced that the touch of soft flesh on the strings better suited the intimacy of the salon. To play with the flesh or with the nails? The difference was like that between a harpsichord and a pianoforte. So with the bare flesh of his thumb, he played the opening phrases of his Opus 28, and then he stopped before the theme. What terrible weather, he thought.

He had played the night before at the salon of Madame Bouchet, a lady whose forcefulness of spirit somewhat outweighed her good taste. His Félicité had been all night at rehearsals for a ballet scheduled for later that December, and he had endured the salon alone, although lately, since they had returned from Moscow it seemed that the time spent at Félicité's side was richer in aloneness than the times when she was absent. There had been something distasteful in the way that Madame Bouchet had treated him the night before, almost as if he was her pet, her lapdog. She had one of those too, an overwrought creature with poor guts who would alternately yap and fart. But the dog had been shunned the previous night whilst all Madame Bouchet's beady attention was lavished upon the guitarist. She had asked him repeatedly to play melodies from Russia and, when he had done so, she had clapped her hands together and squeaked with delight, crying 'How delicious! How barbarous!' When he had finished playing, she had asked him to tell her stories of the sights he had seen, enquired of him whether they really drank spirit made from potatoes (they did, Ferdinand confirmed) and whether—Madame Bouchet was somewhat impressionable by nature—in the forests there were really fairy maidens, as she had heard, who lured travellers off the path (there were none that he knew of). It had, in short, been a trying evening, even if he had made the acquaintance of a number of individuals of good standing and had managed to moot the possibility with one of them of organising a benefit concert some time in the coming weeks; something that, given his somewhat precipitous financial situation, he could well do with.

Already, the return to Paris was proving unsatisfactory. He had hoped that the change of climate would be good for Félicité, that when they moved from Moscow, she might thaw; and indeed she had thawed, only her warmth and vivacity were suppressed when they were together, but whilst when she was in the company of others they were on full display. Ferdinand closed his eyes and played fat chords that resonated on the open strings. That coming night, he was to perform as a soloist at a concert at the Théâtre Orphée. He had no enthusiasm for the idea.

'Father.' It was his daughter, standing by the door. Ferdinand looked round and smiled at her. She was attractive, he thought. Her long dark hair and dark eyes reminded him of the girls he loved back in Spain, when he was just a boy, fresh out of the monastery school. Looking at her, it seemed as if the years that had passed between then and now had been exceptionally long— Paris, London, Berlin, Warsaw, Moscow and again Paris—whilst the years of his childhood were short, as if his whole childhood had taken place in a single day.

His daughter hesitated in the doorway. He wondered whether

she had started to draw the attention of the young men of Paris. 'Come in,' he said.

There was a look of pity on her face. He found her pity hard to bear, so he looked away, towards the window where the rain continued to stream. His daughter sat on a low stool beside the couch. 'Father,' she said, 'are you still sick?'

'A little.'

'You have been drinking brandy.'

'For my health only.'

She lay her head in his lap, her eyes turned away from his, and for a while the two of them listened to the rain batter the window panes.

'You are playing tonight?' she asked.

'I am. Will you be there?'

'Yes, Father. I will be there.'

Ferdinand stroked her hair. He wanted to say something, but he was not sure what. He did not understand his daughter, but he loved her.

'Was Antoine here?' she asked after a while, sitting up.

'Antoine? Yes, he was here.'

His daughter looked thoughtful. Has she fallen for the publisher? he wondered. But then he put the thought to one side. He was tired of second-guessing the hearts of women. What did he know?

The clock struck in the room next door. 'Father, you should get ready. It is already five.'

Ferdinand sat up and attempted a smile. Then he went to get ready for the concert.

37

Three hours later, at the Théâtre Orphée, the red velvet curtains rose, and the audience clapped furiously. There, on the stage, dressed with elegant fastidiousness, was the great guitarist Ferdinand Sor. He stood holding his guitar in his right hand, making short bows. His hair was still thick and he had an air of youthful brilliance to him, yet he was no longer young. His eyes moved across the audience quickly and came to rest on the front row, where his daughter smiled up at him. Beside her, he noted with displeasure, was an empty seat. Félicité was not there. Sor walked to the chair that had been placed centre-stage and arranged himself upon it with care. When he spoke, his French was good, although it was strangely accented—his Spanish origins, his exile in London, his journey to Moscow, all of these things had left their trace in the rhythms of his speech. But it was also a voice that had to it such an extraordinary authority that, had any member of the audience passed by the room where he had been lying prostrate on the couch a few hours earlier, in a fug of sickness, misery and malingering, drinking brandy and feeling sorry for himself, none would have believed that this was the very same man. On stage Ferdinand Sor had an air of a creature who was not subject to human moods, a brilliant figure who might have spent all of his waking hours in a whirl of elegance and refinement, before retiring to a bed of silks and velvet.

'Merci,' he said. 'Je vous remercie,' as he held up a hand to still the audience. Then, when the audience was quiet, he spoke.

'My name is Ferdinand Sor,' he said, although there was no

need to explain this to the crowd, who had come precisely for the privilege of seeing the great guitarist. 'It pleases me greatly to be performing here in Paris once again, after my long exile in London and Moscow.'

He paused, looking over the auditorium. The gas lamps were new since his last performance, and—on those evenings when they refrained from exploding, causing fire and panic—they lent a soft glow to the rows of alternating moustaches and bosoms. The latter of these drew Ferdinand's attention more, and yet there was one bosom that was absent.

'I would like to play you several pieces I wrote whilst on my sojourn in Moscow,' he said. 'I will begin with a Theme and Variations, the melody of which will not, I think, be unfamiliar to you.'

A murmur went through the crowd. Ferdinand checked the tuning of his guitar. Then he started to play. The audience looked puzzled as he entered into the opening phrase, but then as he came to the theme, a murmur of pleasure passed through the audience, for there could have been nobody in that concert hall, from the most well-born to the most humble, who did not know the tune.

Whilst he played, Ferdinand thought of Félicité with such intensity that he was only vaguely aware he was on the stage before an audience of several hundred. His mind was on her, but his fingers were practised and knew what to do; they found their positions on the finger-board without hesitation.

They had met in London in 1822, the young dancer Félicité Hullin and the virtuoso Ferdinand Sor. She had been the lead role in the ballet *Cendrillon*, and had been drawn immediately by his strange mixture of darkness and pallor, by the sorrowfulness of his gaze and by the sweetness of the music he played. For him, it was more simple. For all of his brilliance and his good looks, he was alone, a widower who had nobody

150

with whom to bring up his daughter; and Félicité was young, beautiful, a talented dancer. On the first night that she danced, there in London—the press praised her good legs, and her graceful points and insteps—he knew that he wanted her, that he would not be content unless he could have her.

The early stages of the courtship did not last long. When Félicité received an invitation to dance as first ballerina on the Moscow stage, Ferdinand decided to accompany her, along with his daughter. They left London for Paris, and from there travelled through Berlin and Warsaw, performing at salons and in concert halls along the way. They remained in Moscow until the May of 1826 and at first, there had been nothing in Russia but pleasure and brilliance; but Ferdinand soon became jealous. Félicité, when she was upon the stage, was a thing of wonder. Every movement was fluid and soft, she balanced nobility with agility. Ferdinand found it most unbearable when she danced with Joseph Richard, her fellow countryman; then, it was as if he, Joseph, was everything to her and Ferdinand was nothing. Worse still, were the things that were written in the papers, words that wounded him deeply, likening Félicité and Joseph to the whirlwinds that Descartes claimed were stirred up by the heat of the sun in the fine substance that filled space. How could anyone, the press asked, not imagine that they were in love, with a passion that could outstrip that of all the ancients, the passion of Hero and Leander, of Daphnis and Chlöe? And whilst Joseph had no desire for women, preferring to take his pleasures in the mode of the ancient Greeks—something that was not difficult to do those days in Moscow—the pain of it had nevertheless troubled Ferdinand ever since the very first time he had seen them dance together. It was not that he suspected Félicité of unfaithfulness. Such, with Joseph at least, was far from likely. It was only that when they danced together, their bodies (the accursed journalists wrote) painted wonderful pictures, as if lifted by electric sparks; and Ferdinand felt himself earthbound, knowing that there was some part of his beloved Félicité he could never touch.

All these thoughts ran through his mind as he played, but his fingers did not falter. After the theme came the first variation with its semiquavers that ran like oil, and following this, the brooding second in a minor key, a variation that sent a shudder of unease through the audience, the theme that seemed so light and inconsequential changing into something dark and unsettling. The third variation saved them from this discomfort, a bold, clear restatement of the theme, once again in the major key, giving way to the lyricism of the fourth variation which, although it was played in the major, seemed to be tainted by a memory of the sadness of the minor key. Then the brilliant rippling sextuplets of the fifth and final variation made the audience lean forwards and gape, the moustaches of the men twitching, the bosoms of the women filling out. But just as it seemed that the piece was about to end in this flurry of brilliance, there was a pause, and then a reprise of the melody that had introduced the piece repeated in harmonics that rang bell-like through the concert hall. The final few chords were played with a quiet and wholly unexpected stoicism, so that when the piece came to an end and the musician placed his right hand flat over the sound-hole of the guitar, the audience for a moment seemed wrong-footed, uncertain how to respond. Then there was the sound of heavy clapping. Somebody cried 'Bravo!' and then, as is the way with crowds, the mood shifted, several people rose, the cries of 'Bravo!' increased in number and intensity, and in a moment the whole of the audience of the Théâtre Orphée surged upwards from their seats, and the applause thundered. Ferdinand stood to take a bow, smiling wanly; but all he could think of was the empty place in the front row next to where his daughter, his dear daughter, was seated.

38

As the winter progressed, it was as if Paris belonged to Ferdinand alone. His first concert was so well received that the doors of society were flung open to him. If he had enjoyed success before, it had never approached this level of adulation. Yet as the weather grew colder and ever more wretched, Ferdinand found himself settling into a deeper and deeper gloom. He saw little of Félicité, and on those occasions that they shared a bed, their love-making was cursory and hollow. Most of the time, he stayed in his room by the fire, lying on the couch and staring up at the ceiling. His daughter attended him as best she could. Occasionally Antoine arrived to say smoothly that the Maison Meissonnier was most pleased with the sales of the manuscript edition. Other than this, his days were spent alone. It was as if there were two Ferdinands that winter—the Ferdinand who brooded upon his couch, unkempt and bedraggled, and the glittering composer and virtuoso who, night after night, dressed immaculately for the occasion, stunned the audiences of Paris with the passion and fervour of his music. It would be a temptation, no doubt, to claim that the former Ferdinand, the couch-dweller, was the true Ferdinand, and the latter the false Ferdinand; and yet anyone who attended the concerts would have found this implausible, because there was nothing false about the way that this man played. There was, when he performed, no trace of a mask; nor was there as he glided through the crowds, talking smoothly to the society ladies, laughing and joking, telling tales of life in Moscow and London, or of his early days when he fought the armies of Napoleon. These two Ferdinands inhabited different worlds, and it was possible to imagine that, had they ever met and found themselves standing together in the same room, forced to make conversation, they would have had virtually nothing to say to each other.

It was on a Saturday morning in early February that there was a knock upon Ferdinand's door. He sent his daughter down to answer it, feeling disinclined towards keeping the company of others. She returned several moments later. 'There is a man outside who speaks in German,' she said. 'He looks like a vagrant: his clothes are poor and torn, and he was shivering in the cold. He has with him a guitar. He brought you a letter.' She handed Ferdinand the envelope.

The guitarist opened the envelope and scanned through the page. It was written in French, and signed Karl Toepfer. The name was familiar, but it was a moment or two before he remembered: a guitarist of moderate talents from Vienna, and a philosopher of no greater ability, if rumour was to be believed, with whom Ferdinand had exchanged something of a tiresome correspondence several years ago. Ferdinand's eyes returned to the beginning of the letter. Toepfer, in courteous and well-honed phrases, asked that the bearer, a M. Gelski by name, might be taken on as a pupil, in light of his 'not inconsiderable talent'; he went on to say that although the pupil would be unable to pay for the guitarist's services, Ferdinand, were he to agree, would certainly be richly rewarded by the muses, who had jurisdiction over all the arts.

Ferdinand sighed and folded the letter several times over. 'Has the man departed?' he asked his daughter.

'He is waiting by the door for your answer. You can see for yourself if you look from the window.'

Ferdinand took a couple of steps towards the window and

looked down. There, in the street outside, was a strange, shambling figure. A turban of rags was wrapped around his head, the remainder of his clothing a tattered and worn patchwork of fur and fabric. On his face was a thick beard, and his eyes were so deep-set that it seemed that the sockets contained only darkness. Ferdinand shuddered. There was something unearthly about the figure that stood, eyes lowered, in the road beneath his window. The man's feet were almost bare, despite the coldness of the season. On his back was slung a guitar. There was something in the way that he stood there, as if he might stand there forever waiting to be admitted, that made Ferdinand fearful. 'Tell the beggar I have no time to take on pupils,' Ferdinand told his daughter. He turned from the window. 'Tell him,' he said, a little more quietly, 'to leave me in peace.'

His daughter left the room, and Ferdinand heard her quick footsteps disappear down the stairs. He watched from the window, and could see the visitor rocking his head from side to side as they conversed; but his daughter's voice was inaudible. Then he heard the door close. The visitor rolled his shoulders and crossed the street, where he sat down on a low wall. Ferdinand stepped back into the darkness.

His daughter returned to the room not long after. 'He is gone,' she said.

'On the contrary,' Ferdinand said. 'He is waiting outside.' He pointed towards where the man was sitting, unmoving on the wall, his eyes slightly lowered.

By mid-afternoon, the petitioner was still there, despite the sleet that had started up around noon. When Ferdinand looked again after dark, he could see the shape of the man still hunched across the street. He had not moved from where he had seated himself that morning.

That night, the Spaniard slept badly. Twice he woke and walked to the window, and saw that the visitor was still there, stoic and impassive in the moonlight. And when the guitarist woke again, just before dawn, he looked from the window again, hoping that the foreigner might have departed, only to be disappointed. It was Sunday morning. The sun came up without enthusiasm; and Ferdinand, lacking any desire for breakfast, tried occupying himself with reading. But it was no use. He could not help himself from going to the window every few moments to check if the man was still there. It was only when the church bells started ringing, some time in the mid-morning, that the figure stood up from where he had been keeping his vigil and, his guitar upon his back, without looking up at the window from where Ferdinand was watching, turned and disappeared down the street.

When he had gone, Ferdinand took the letter from Toepfer and fed it into the fire. Then he wrapped a blanket around his shoulders, hunched himself up, and looked into the flames with a melancholy gaze.

39

That Michot and Blanchard, two respectable society men, should have been on the hill of Montmartre on a snowy February night is something that is itself a cause for puzzlement. This was not a district in which one would have expected to have found those of good name. This was a time long before the great church sprang up from the top of the hill as white as a mushroom in a summer field, when the narrow streets were occupied by the dispossessed and desperate, by gamblers and drunks soaked in the wine sold by the Benedictine Sisters, by scoundrels and thugs and footpads and cutpurses. But Michot and Blanchard were men known for their probity and their good standing, and their presence there in Montmartre remains something of a mystery.

Blanchard, whom we should properly call Doctor Blanchard, was a physician by training and had written an influential text on the use of certain techniques of breathing for the cure of ailments peculiar to the weaker sex. Michot was the owner of a small theatre, the imposingly named Grand Théâtre de Montmartre, which stood at the foot of the hill of Montmartre, not so far from the Orphée, although the Grand Théâtre was known to attract a lower class of audience. Well-dressed and delicate in demeanour, the two men made their way through the dark streets. They had been friends since childhood, had played together in the street, had suffered their schooling side by side, and had in the process developed the kind of friendship and affection that continues to endure through force of habit and shared history, in the face of the multitudinous differences of their temperaments and the absence of much in the way of mutual interest.

They were walking through the district immediately surrounding the church of Saint-Pierre, and for all we know it may be that they climbed the hill simply to pay their respects to that Rock upon which the Church is founded, to offer up prayers and pieties, their chins buried in their coats to keep warm, their boots becoming soaked through by the cold snow. Whatever the business on the hill, as they started to descend to the city below, they heard, coming from some place not far off, the most extraordinary music. To Michot, who had a fair knowledge of music, it sounded as if these melodies and harmonies had about them something of the Orient, something of the reek of cloves and nutmeg and spices. Doctor Blanchard, on the other hand, had what are properly called cloth ears. To him all music was much the same—for here was a man who could not tell which pitch was lower and which was higher, even if they were a whole two octaves apart, an impairment that went beyond the bounds of reason and comprehension, becoming itself became a cause for astonished comment. Michot held up his hand to Blanchard and said, 'Wait, listen!' Blanchard did as he was told without gaining anything of significance thereby. But Michot's head was tilted to one side, and he seemed to almost sniff the air as the snow fell around him in large, wet flakes. 'Come,' he said to his friend. 'Let us see who is playing.'

Uneasily, Blanchard followed Michot into the alleyway from which the music was coming. If it had been up to him, he would have made his way down the hill as quickly as possible to where the streets were illuminated by gas lights; but he feared walking through those winding streets alone, and so he could do nothing other than follow his friend, who went ahead down the side alley that led from darkness into even thicker darkness. As they drew closer, the unsettled rhythms of this strange music put Doctor Blanchard on edge. Blanchard's feeling for rhythm was, all things considered, rather more advanced than his feeling for pitch; and this jagged, uneven measure seemed to Blanchard to be close to the unsteady breathing of those patients he cured with his method: the hysterical, the hay-feverish, the frenetic, the distressed, the asthmatic. The rhythms came in uneven gasps: one-two, one-two, one-two-three, one-two; one-two, one-two, one-two-three, one-two. Blanchard followed the small, retreating back of Michot down the alley, tugging anxiously at his own beard as he did so.

They came out into a little square that was lit by the weak light streaming from a lamp that was set in an upstairs window. Hunched on a step in the darkness was a figure swaddled in rags. A man, no doubt, but a man who seemed to gather the dark around him as he sat in the snow on the step, a man who seemed to be both there and to be not there, to be both visible and somehow darker than the night that surrounded him. He was, it was clear, a vagrant. His feet were bound in strips of cloth—he had no shoes—and large, gnarled toes poked out into the cold night air. Around his shoulders was a rough blanket, and on his head he wore rags twisted into a kind of turban. Just beneath the turban was a face that looked, in that light at least, to be closer to that of a beast than of a man: a dark furring of hair and beard; a snarling mouth. The monster's eyes were closed, and in his hands was a guitar that he was playing with astonishing savagery, wrenching the music from the guitar's body in jagged, unpredictable rhythms. Blanchard immediately desired to be elsewhere, to be unlocking the door of his apartment and closing it behind him, to be warming himself by the fire whilst his good, patient wife served him something hot and restorative to drink. He tried to draw Michot away, terrified that, having led them into this dark square by means of the strange charms of his music, this vagrant would set upon them with a knife and destroy them utterly; but his friend was standing transfixed, swaying as the snow fell around him, a small smile on his pale face.

'Michot,' whispered the doctor, 'let us leave. It is not safe.'

Michot lifted a hand lightly to quieten his friend. And when Blanchard looked at him again, he knew what that smile meant. He had seen it before. Always the same smile, and it always meant the same thing: money. For if Michot was a lover of music, he loved money with an even greater fervour; and times lately had been hard, with the return of that Spaniard Sor from Moscow, who filled the Orphée and, in the process, deprived every other theatre in Paris of custom. It had, in fact, been this very hardship that had inspired Michot to climb the hill at Montmartre in the first place, so that he might find some sop for his sorrows in the back alleys. And now, by some magnificent chance, he had stumbled across a spectacle that could once again fill his theatre and thus his pockets. All of this Blanchard could read in his friend's face, because those who love money more than all else are, in the end, without a great degree of subtlety, there being no complex moral calculus that might stand between their desires and the hope of their fulfilment.

'Michot,' Blanchard said again, not only because he was afraid of this man who crouched in the shadows playing his strange, demonic music, but also because he was beginning to feel the cold seeping through his boots and his stockings to his flesh, and through his flesh to his very bones beneath.

The musician seemed to realise that he was being watched. He ended the phrase abruptly and took his right hand from the guitar, allowing the strings to ring out. He turned his head and looked up at the two men who stood no more than twenty paces away. But when he spoke, his voice was gentle, even though neither man could understand the language he spoke.

Michot took a few steps forwards until his face was in the light coming from the upstairs window. He took off his hat, a gesture of courtesy 'Excuse me,' he said, 'my name is Michot.'

The man did not move. He looked up at the theatre owner. 'Misho?' he said.

The name sounded somehow coarse in the foreigner's mouth. 'Michot,' repeated the theatre owner. He crouched down so that he was squatting on his haunches, and held out his hand the way one might tempt a recalcitrant dog to come and take some scraps of food. 'My name,' he repeated, 'is Michot. Do you understand me?'

The man spoke hesitantly. 'Deutsch? Ich kann Deutsch sprechen.' The words tumbled awkwardly onto the snowy ground.

Michot, who knew no German, but who, with his gift for music, easily recognised the precise cadences of the language, turned to Blanchard for help. 'Doctor Blanchard,' he said, 'come translate for us.'

Blanchard sighed and stepped forward to join his friend. 'Ask him his name,' Michot told him. 'Get him to tell me his name.'

The doctor put the question in German, but the question was met at first with silence, the vagrant staring down at the ground, as if thinking deeply.

Blanchard would have repeated the question, had fear not made him hesitate. But the stranger had both heard and understood. At length he looked up at Blanchard and, in a voice free of any trace of emotion, each syllable ponderous and equally weighted, 'Mein Name ist Ivan Gelski.'

40

Having spoken his name, the vagrant seemed little inclined to speak any further. Blanchard, at Michot's prompting, asked the stranger where he had come from, and the stranger simply said, 'Far away.' Asked where he learned the guitar, the stranger muttered 'Wien,' and then was convulsed by a tubercular cough that shook his entire body. He turned his head and spat, and something dark landed in the snow. Then he looked down at his bare toes. Now that they were close, Michot and Blanchard could see that the man's toes were chapped and swollen with sores. The bandages were filthy. When Blanchard asked him if he had a home, he did not reply at all, perhaps because of the coughing and perhaps because he did not know how to answer.

Michot glanced at Blanchard. 'We must take him in,' he said in French. 'Tell him that we are taking him to some warm rooms, where we will give him food. And brandy. We will prepare a hot bath, and you can tend to his wounds. Then, when this is done, we will give him new clothes.'

Blanchard smiled. 'Monsieur Michot,' he said, 'your charity is unusual.'

'As is this man's talent,' Michot replied. 'Do not worry, I will pay you for your services. I know that doctors, too, have to eat.'

Blanchard relayed the substance of Michot's intentions to the vagrant.

Ivan Gelski did not respond. He seemed somehow turned

inward, as if listening to a music that only he could hear.

'Come,' said Michot, 'Let us help him to his feet.'

Doctor Blanchard looked at his friend uneasily. 'Perhaps we should wait for his assent,' he said.

Michot was impatient. 'Ask him again,' he said. 'No. Tell him. Tell him that we are taking him somewhere warm and safe. Tell him that if he does not want to accompany us, he should speak. Otherwise, he can remain silent.'

Blanchard translated, but the man remained as motionless and unresponsive as a block of granite.

'Come, then, let us waste no more time. I am cold, and I too could do with a brandy.' Michot stepped forward. 'Come on,' he said in French to the man sitting in the snow. 'We're taking you in. You'll die out here.' He reached out and touched the arm of the stranger.

The response was immediate and unexpected. The man reached over his guitar and grabbed the theatre owner by the collar so that he lost his footing on the icy ground of the square and fell awkwardly to his knees. Still grasping Michot's collar, the stranger leaned over so that the theatre owner could smell the rankness of the foreigner's breath, the smell of unwashed skin. The stranger muttered a couple of sentences in heavily accented German.

'What is he saying?' Michot gasped. 'Tell me what he is saying.'

'He says that he will come with you,' Blanchard translated, 'and he will accept your hospitality. But if you cheat him, he will kill you.'

Michot's expression showed that he understood. Ivan grunted once and let go. Then he turned and strummed a few chords on the guitar. This seemed to soothe him. Almost instantly, a look of calm returned to his face. He looked up at Doctor Blanchard and spoke a few more rough words. 'He can hardly walk,'

Blanchard said. 'He is sick. He will need help.'

Michot seemed hesitant, as if he was no longer certain that he wanted to take this stranger into his care and keeping; but the offer had been made and Michot reminded himself that whatever difficulties there might be would be counterbalanced by the promise of considerable profit. He was already considering what he would write in the programme notes, the reports in the press, the receipts at the end of the evening. It was not that Michot was without compassion, nor was it that money was the only route to his heart; it was merely that of all the routes, the financial was the most direct and the most efficient. And so, keeping in mind the possibility of future profit, and at the same time reminding himself that it was not Blanchard who had strayed off the path on this cold February night in one of the less salubrious districts of Montmartre, but he himself, he bowed to necessity and placed the right arm of the stranger around his shoulder, something that the stranger permitted him to do with good enough grace.

Blanchard attempted to take the guitar from Ivan's hands so that he could take the other arm; but the musician held on to it fast, and so with Ivan relying only on Michot for support, the three men started to make their way out of the square.

41

It was slow going. Only when they got the man to his feet did it become apparent quite how sick he was. He wheezed as he walked, muttering to himself in whatever language it was that he spoke. Michot was neither particularly strong nor particularly tall; and as they hobbled through the square back to the alley that would lead to the road down the hill, the burden on Michot's shoulders seemed not merely physical, but also a weight of sorrow, of rage and of suffering. Every step that Michot took, he winced to see the swollen and half-bare feet of the stranger as they trudged through the snow.

Ivan shuddered and muttered occasionally, but did not put up any more of a fight. The three men walked through the scant light under the three-quarters moon that was reflected by the snow. To those who passed by, it must have looked as if these were three friends who had gone drinking and carousing up on the hill, far from their homes and their wives, and were now making their way home, the drunkest of the party with his arm around another for support.

As they walked, Doctor Blanchard was silent, walking beside them with a thoughtful look on his face. Doctors always have their preoccupations and their concerns. They spend their days with sickness and death, touching the bodies of others in strange, intimate rituals of healing. They have a lot on their minds. Blanchard was thinking about the man's feet; and not only his feet, but the tubercular cough and the sickness that showed in his face. He was thinking about infection and sores and poultices and parasites and patent lotions and the papers that he had read in the latest scientific journals and the possibility of breathing-cures. He was thinking about the distance to a street where they might be able to hail a carriage, about frostbite, about the snow that was continuing to fall around them, about when he might, at last, return home to his wife and get some sleep.

The streets were almost deserted, save for a few drunks lurching their way homeward and a man who hurried past in the robes of a priest. The three men stood by the side of the road for a few moments, the foreigner Ivan wheezing, his left arm wrapped around his guitar, the right around Michot's shoulder. 'Where do you propose to take him?' asked the doctor.

'I have a room in my apartment. It has a fireplace and a bed, and he will be comfortable enough. He will be well looked after by Madame Carnot. She is a capable woman.'

Unlike the doctor, Michot had no wife to contend with, and thus such decisions were relatively easily made. Madame Carnot, his housekeeper, was a widow whom he paid a small stipend in return for her unexceptional labours. Madame Carnot was a poor cook—Michot liked to joke that her husband had died of poisoning—and was even poorer at keeping house; but she was not a gossip, and this was of importance to Michot who was committed to retaining the privacy of his domestic realm. In truth, the reason for her failure to gossip was not that Madame Carnot was of a particularly discreet nature, but rather that she had few friends, if any, that she could take into her confidence. And so, although she might disapprove of the new arrival—as she surely would, for she disapproved of almost everything—she would not speak of him to others; and Michot had already calculated that it would be of considerable value if his new discovery could be kept secret as long as possible, so that on being announced to society, the announcement might be accompanied by an aura of mystery that would contribute significantly to the takings. The thought of sharing his house with this man, this beast who had wrestled him to his knees (he could feel the beginnings of an incipient bruise on his right shin where it had struck a protruding cobble-stone) did not much appeal to him; but once again he reminded himself of the potential profits that awaited, and thus he was a little reassured.

There was a clattering from down the street, and a cab appeared out of the gloom. Blanchard stepped out to hail it. The horses came to an impatient halt, and he helped the sick man into the cab. 'We must pass by my office,' he said. 'I must collect my bag to treat the patient. Then we can repair to your apartment and see what is to be done.'

The three men climbed into the cab and closed the door. The coachman muttered under his breath and snapped his whip.

42

It was dawn by the time that Ivan had been put to sleep with the assistance of several doses of brandy and morphine. Madame Carnot had been awake when Michot and Blanchard arrived back at the apartment. Didn't the old bird ever sleep? Michot wondered. She was awake every morning before he was and always retired after he did, whatever time he returned, if only for the pleasure of huffing and puffing to herself about the lateness of the hour that he arrived home.

They had administered the first dose of morphine and brandy early on, shortly after arriving at Michot's apartment. They came in and lit the fire and Michot asked Madame Carnot to heat water for a bath, but as Michot and Blanchard had tried to gently ease the guitar from the patient's grasp, he had begun to struggle. It took morphine, alcohol and Blanchard's soothing manner to pacify him. They placed the guitar carefully in the corner of the room where the wooden top reflected the flickering light of the fire, then they made the patient comfortable on a couch, being careful first to cover the fabric with a sheet, for the man's clothes were filthy and who knows what parasites he was carrying? They started with his feet. Already the morphine was making Ivan's head loll.

It was an unpleasant job cutting the filthy bandages from the patient's feet. Ivan slipped in and out of consciousness as Blanchard did his skilled work with the scissors. When he had cut the last of the rags free, he could see that the man's feet were in a terrible state, gnarled and malodorous, and running with pus and clear, filmy liquid. It was as if he had walked all the way from Vienna without shoes. Or perhaps his shoes had been stolen. There were people cruel enough, or desperate enough, to steal the shoes of another man. The skin between the toes was cracked; it burned and pulsed with an angry red through the thick covering of grime. The soles and heels were covered with blisters that had become infected. Michot carefully swabbed the feet clean with brandy. Soon fragments of pink skin appeared. Somehow, there was no frostbite, although how he had managed to avoid it was anyone's guess.

Comfrey, he muttered to Michot. He had learned this cure from an English doctor a decade before—it was recommended in an old herbal written at the time of Queen Elizabeth—and it had proved remarkably efficacious. Revolutionary though his method of curing ailments of the body by means of the judicious practice of modulated breathing was, Blanchard was a good enough physician to recognise that it was not suited to all forms of bodily disease. Hot poultices of comfrey, applied to the feet every morning and night, would draw out the poison from the system. But first the sores would need to be lanced, a simple enough job. After taking the precaution of administering a further few drops of morphine, Blanchard performed the lancing by prodding at the sores with a fine needle, and he wiped the pus away with a cloth as it oozed out, deep yellow in the gas light. The remainder he squeezed out until there was no more yellow, only the healthy red of clean blood.

After they had cleared up the worst of the mess of the man's feet, Madame Carnot came in to say that the bath was ready. Blanchard and Michot hauled the man to his feet. He was only half-conscious, but the messages of pain from his feet were still finding their way through the fug of opiates to his brain, and from time to time, as they took him into the bath-chamber, he muttered and tossed his head. There, with the help of Madame Carnot (who, at this point, had to struggle to keep in check the rapid beating of her heart) they removed the man's clothes, if the rags he was wearing, layer upon layer of rags, were fit to be called clothes. Before long he was naked, and for all Madame Carnot's excitement, she put up a convincing display of indifference. Together, they lifted him into the bath, and then they scrubbed his body until the water was covered in a thick layer of scum and the flesh emerged from the covering of filth, looking strangely innocent, like that of a newborn, except for the wound, long-healed, in the man's thigh that Doctor Blanchard recognised immediately as being that of a bullet. The patient was barely conscious, and when they soaped his beard and hair, he hardly seemed to notice. Michot asked Madame Carnot to bring some clothes and, although he himself was of considerably slighter build than the stranger, they found a nightshirt that sufficed well enough. Removing him from the bath, Michot and Blanchard held the foreigner whist Madame Carnot patted him dry, and then they slipped the nightshirt upon him. Seeing him dressed like that made the housekeeper want to giggle: he looked so child-like and so lost, his head tipping to one side, his mouth open in a morphine daze, and yet he had such a powerful presence, that she was quite overwhelmed with a curious kind of affection for the man. She turned her face away so that the two other men would not see her smile. 'Madame Carnot,' Blanchard said, 'is the bed prepared?'

Madame Carnot gave a little curtsey and scurried out of the room. They seated the man in a bath chair and waited for her to return, which she did only a few moments later. 'All is ready,' she said.

'Thank you, Madame Carnot,' said Michot. 'You may retire.'

'Of course,' she said, and she ducked out of the room—but

not to sleep. She remained awake and vigilant in her rooms, keeping her keen ears on the noises that came through the door, not wanting to miss anything. Her tendency to rise early and to sleep late was not born out of diligence so much as out of an almost pathological curiosity about that comings and goings in the household; and if she was not, by force of circumstance, a gossip, it was also probably true that, should the opportunity ever have presented itself to enter into this kind of confidence with another, she would have stories enough to tell.

When they had him laid in the bed, Blanchard got to work with the comfrey poultices on the feet—he always carried dried leaves of comfrey in his bag, and these could be invigorated by a little warm water mixed with brandy (what a useful drug brandy was, he thought; what a benefit to all mankind). The situation was not as grave as he had feared. Other than a few minor infections, insect bites, and the bullet wound that had healed many years before, the man's body had not suffered too much. He would surely live. There was the cough, of course, but that could be easily treated. The foreigner's body was still robust; there was still strength enough in him; the comfrey would do the work on the infected feet. But it is lucky, he thought, that they had found him. He knew how quickly poison goes to the blood, and is then carried to every corner of the body. When that happens, no cure, no comfrey or brandy or modulated breathing, can assist the sufferer, and death is, barring a miracle, all but certain.

Michot watched him work on the poultices. Blanchard felt his eyes upon him. 'What are you going to do with this stranger in your house?' Blanchard asked.

'I will care for him, I will pay for your services as doctor.'

'And translator,' Blanchard smiled as he laid another strip of the herb on the man's feet.

Michot laughed. 'Of course,' he said. 'And translator.'

171

'And then? Then you will exploit him?'

'Then,' Michot said, 'I will make him a rich man. I shall put him on the stage; and he will play music the like of which Paris has never before heard. Since that Spaniard returned from Moscow, my theatre has been empty and the seats in the Orphée are filled. This situation cannot be endured.'

'You presume I will help you in this?'

'Bertrand,' said Michot, addressing his friend by his first name, as if he were his brother, 'I know you will help me, because you are a good man.'

Bertrand Blanchard glanced at the theatre owner, but did not say anything.

'You care too much for the welfare of mankind. You will help me, Bertrand, because without my care, this man would have died tonight.'

The doctor looked out of the window at the sky which was now beginning to fade to a dawn heavy with oppressive brown cloud. The snow was continuing to fall in heavy flakes. And he knew that what his friend said was true.

43

The following days were curious ones for Michot. The patient's health improved steadily. Madame Carnot attended him with uncommon courtesy and diligence as he lay in his bed drinking hot restorative broth; and whilst Ivan was calm and quiet for Madame Carnot, when Michot entered the room, the patient sat up in his bed and growled. Michot kept his distance, allowing Madame Carnot to go about her business, relieved that the patient was still bed-bound. He still remembered the way the man had grabbed his collar, the sheer ferocity of his grip; and he was haunted by the thought that this was a man who could kill him if he chose. Michot imagined that beneath the foreigner's skin there coursed a molten river of fury, as in certain countries known for their volcanic activity; and he had enough of a sense of self-preservation not to provoke him, indeed to have, for the time being, as little to do with him as he could.

Blanchard came every day bearing fresh sprigs of comfrey, to change the patient's dressings and to speak with him. Ivan tolerated Blanchard's visits uncomplainingly, replying to the doctor's questions in brief, heavily accented German. They did not spend long in conversation, for the guest seemed taciturn by nature. What it was possible to establish was that he came from the Rhodope hills in the Ottoman lands to the south of the Danube—the home, Blanchard noted, having read widely in the classics, of Orphée—and that he had studied the guitar in Vienna. He would say no more than this, and for Blanchard it was enough. The detail about Orphée was naturally pleasing to Michot, who knew that classical allusion was flattering to the public, and who liked the idea of outdoing the Théâtre Orphée with an Orpheus of his own. He could already see the handbills printed for the concert—'M. Gelski, from the land of Orpheus...', and the thought made him smile. When the public are flattered, without having any great intellectual demands put upon them, their purses spring open with an almost magical ease.

Michot left Blanchard to it whilst he tended the patient, and when Blanchard had done so, Michot asked him whether he would be so kind as to take the patient's measurements, so that these could be sent to a tailor he knew and trusted, to get several good-quality suits of clothing made up—three for everyday wear, and two for performance. Little more than a week later, the suits arrived. Michot smiled as he looked at the fine weave of the fabric. A worthwhile investment.

For most of his convalescence, Ivan lay quietly in his bed, gazing from the window; but at times, he became agitated. At night he would cry out, and several times Michot woke up to the disconcerting sound of violent weeping coming from his house-guest's room; but at other times, Michot would smile to hear sweeter sounds. As his wounds started to heal and the sickness in his chest subsided, Ivan picked up the guitar more often, and played sweet, savage music. Michot would crouch on the other side of the guest's door, trembling with a mixture of fear and excitement as he heard the guitarist play.

Everything about the foreigner's music was extraordinary. His guitar was tuned to a strange key, and the melodies he played—striking the strings with ferocity with his bear-like claws—seemed, to Michot's ears, barbaric: melodies as far as was possible from those popular tunes 'alla Turc', those follies and divertimenti so beloved of the composers of the previous half-century, who dreamed of harems and camel trains and caravanserais where men smoked opium and gazed into the flames. Michot could well believe that these melodies that he was hearing as he pressed his ear to the guitarist's door were the tunes that Orphée himself played, tunes that could enrage or could pacify, tunes that were forever bound up with the strange and savage retinue of Dionysus. Yet there was something else in the music as well, something Viennese, something Apollonian, an orderliness that pulled in the opposing direction to the Orphic strains. At times it was possible to hear echoes of Viennese society music, music that, once polite, had now become feral and undomesticated.

Yet what fascinated Michot most were the time signatures, signatures which seemed almost beyond calculation: 7/8, 11/8, 13/8—time signatures that marched up the strange mathematical progression of prime numbers. The more he listened, the more he admired his guest's music; but his admiration was tainted by fear: the kind of fear that one might experience whilst admiring an animal stretching itself behind the bars of an enclosure in the zoological gardens. Yet there were no bars protecting Michot from the savage in his house, and the thought unsettled him, put him on edge. Whenever the music stopped, he quietly rose from his listening post outside the door and crept away down the corridor.

February turned to March, and the snows melted. Blue and yellow crocuses and white snowdrops pushed up through the ground, and the trees filled with the song of birds marking their territories. The dressings had now come off the patient's feet, and he was no longer consigned to bed. Ivan stayed mainly in his room, where Madame Carnot served him with food. On those rare occasions he crossed Michot's path, the theatre owner stepped to one side whilst Ivan passed, muttering under his breath. Now that he was back on his feet and cleaned up, dressed in good clothes, his guest was an impressive sight. He was gaining in weight a little, thanks to the broth, from which he had graduated to solid foods. The ruddiness in his cheeks returned. He was a handsome man, Michot noted, and his beard was striking. A marketable commodity, that is to say, certain to cause a sensation amongst the women.

Some time before the middle of the month of March, Blanchard came to visit to check on the health of the patient; and, after a thorough examination to which Ivan submitted without any protest, he proclaimed that Ivan was in full health.

'He is ready to perform, then?' Michot asked.

'Have you asked him if he wishes to do so?'

Michot hesitated. 'He will perform,' he said. 'If he does not, then I shall expel him from my house, and have no more to do with him.'

Blanchard looked at his old friend steadily, but said nothing in reply. 'Come,' said Michot. 'I have something to show you.' He led the doctor into his office and took out a piece of paper. 'A contract,' he said. 'I have drawn it up with the assistance of an acquaintance who is skilled in legal matters. All that is required is that you translate it into German, and explain it to Monsieur Gelski. If he agrees, then we will sign it today. It is a fair contract. My initial proposal is for eight concerts, two a week, over a period of one month. I will have sole responsibility for presenting our guest to the public. After one month has passed, if things are going well we will extend the contract, and I will consider the possibility of publishing his music in manuscript form. I shall also ensure that there is suitable accommodation for Monsieur Gelski, now that he is recovered, at an alternative location. It is troublesome having him in my household. He is not the most friendly of guests.' Michot smiled for a moment, then returned to the matter in hand. 'The contract is binding for a month, and for no longer. There are no hidden clauses.' He held the contract in the air in his right hand and looked Blanchard in the eye. 'As for financial arrangements, we will divide fifty per cent of profits between us, half to my account and half to Monsieur Gelski. Unless, of course, you would also like a small proportion out of consideration for your kindness.'

'A small proportion, presumably to be taken out of Monsieur Gelski's share?' asked Blanchard, raising an eyebrow.

'Naturally,' said Michot. 'I am a businessman, and I cannot afford to take less than fifty per cent.'

'In which case, I will refrain,' said Blanchard.

'But you are willing to translate it for me?'

'Let me see,' said Blanchard. Michot handed him the contract and he looked through it. There was nothing in it to which any signatory could object. 'I will translate it, yet I suspect that Monsieur Gelski is not a man who to be bound by contractual obligations.'

Michot looked surprised. 'But, my friend, everybody is bound by contractual obligations. It is the way of the world.'

Blanchard leaned forwards. 'You should be careful,' he said. 'Perhaps Monsieur Gelski is the kind of man who knows only one kind of contract.'

'And what kind of contract is that?'

'The kind which requires no signature: the contract of honour of one who is generous to friends, but who does not hesitate to cut the throats of those who betray.'

Michot laughed.

Blanchard remained unsmiling and serious. 'Give me a pen and paper,' he said, 'and I will start my translation.'

44

Ivan did not protest when Blanchard read the contract, took the guitarist's thumb, pressed it into a cloth soaked with ink, and them made its mark upon the bottom of the paper.

'Your first concert…' Michot said to Ivan, and then—because Blanchard did not take the initiative himself—he turned to Blanchard and nodded at him to prompt a translation, '… your first concert will be the following week. It will be a benefit concert. You will be playing alongside some of the greatest performers in Paris.'

Blanchard translated as Michot spoke about terms and conditions and obligations and responsibilities and termination clauses and subsidiary clauses; meanwhile Ivan just stared down at the black mark upon his thumb, frowning at the way that the ink followed the whorls and the loops, grunting every so often in a fashion that made Michot uneasy.

When Michot had finished, he politely asked Ivan's leave, and he and Blanchot left the guitarist alone. Ivan stood and walked over to the window to look out over the rooftops of Paris. He loosened his collar a little. The stiff, formal clothes that Misho had made for him seemed constraining. Outside, a cat was lying asleep in the sun. A gaggle of pigeons squabbled for scraps down on the pavement. Every so often there was a racket of coach-wheels and horses' hooves at the end of the street. The doctor is kind, Ivan thought. He is kind and he is gentle and his heart is good. He has about him the look of a scholar or a priest. He is trustworthy. The other man, the one called Misho, is different. He is a man like the merchants who passed through the mountains, not caring for their servants or their companions or their horses, nor even for themselves, but only for money. Ivan had killed many men of that kind; but he did not want to kill again. It was true that he did not like the way Misho looked at him, as if he was a cow or a horse or something to be traded; he did not like the way that he could hear the man listening outside the door as he played his music; he did not like the way that the man held himself, the way his eyes seemed to slide away from holding the gaze; but what Ivan feared above all else was that Misho might betray him, and that in the heat of betrayal the rage might come flooding back into his own heart. What he feared was the very same thing that Misho feared: that one day soon, he might find himself running a knife across the theatre owner's throat.

Then his thoughts turned to the past. As a rule, Ivan did not think much upon the past. But this morning, as he stood gazing out of the window, all the springtimes he had lived through returned to him: the yellow cherry blossom, the rivers and streams swelled with snowmelt, the voice of his mother singing softly at the loom, the roughness of his father's hands, that morning when he left his sick bed and headed into the mountains to meet with Bogdan Voyvoda, the first kill of the season, the nights by the fire whilst the gaidar played and rakiya was passed around. He remembered those few, brief springtimes in Vienna, the kindness of Toepfer, the way the mist hung over the Danube. And he thought of how, at this very moment, the upland meadows at home would be blossoming, how it was at precisely this time of year, perhaps on this very day, that he once would have taken off his monk's robes and rolled them up, leaving the monastery in Skopje with several months of cold bitterness in his heart, to return home to the mountains. And for a moment, Ivan Gelski felt nothing but a great, vast hollowness that seemed to suck everything of meaning and significance: the cat, the pigeons, the coach-wheels and horses' hooves, the dark inky smudge upon his thumb, the perpetual attentions of the housekeeper, Misho, Blanchard, Paris, the guitar, even music itself. All of it worth nothing. Worth nothing at all. But then in this great and hollow darkness he detected something else, the trace of a melody, something that was not other than the darkness, but that was a thread running through it, a thread that offered the promise that darkness might be capable of redeeming itself. And the image of Stoyanka returned to him.

During the years since he left the village of Gela—for all the time that he had hidden out in the hills, spilling the blood of men, for the long winter months in the monastery, whilst he had been an exile in Vienna—her image had become so faint that he sometimes found himself asking what colour her eyes had been; yet for a moment, there at the window of the apartment in Paris, it was as if she was standing before him. It was not so much an image as a sense of her presence: the shape of her soul revealed, momentarily, to his own soul. The shock of the remembrance was so great that he had to grasp hold of the window sill to avoid falling to the ground. Then the cat got up and stretched, the pigeons took flight and Ivan turned away from the window.

His hand reached out for reassurance towards his guitar, and he played sad melodies until Madame Carnot entered to say that his dinner was served.

45

Ivan had left Vienna on the Danube in mid-autumn the previous year, just as the air was beginning to become cold, taking with him the guitar that had once belonged to Solomon. And because he had never developed the taste for travelling by coach, he departed on foot, his guitar upon his back. He wished Karl Toepfer and his wife farewell, embraced the two children, of whom he had become fond, and left behind the city that, like Narcissus, gazed perpetually at its own image as it was reflected in the waters of the Danube. When he was clear of the city, he settled down for the night, lighting a small fire, and gazing up at the stars. He shivered as he looked into the flames. I have become soft, he said to himself. In all these years living in the city, I have become soft. Then, after playing for a while to soothe his heart and to warm his body, for the first time in years, he slept out in the open air.

After Ivan's departure, Toepfer took no more pupils, nor did he perform on the guitar in public again. He took his own guitar, removed its six strings, polished it carefully, and stowed it away. A few days later, he sat down at his desk, took out a pen, and set to work on the project that would preoccupy him for the remainder of his days: a monumental history of the guitar. The work, which Toepfer called *The Descent of the Lyre*, was never completed; however the manuscript now resides in the university library at Tübingen. It is written in a hasty and sometimes illegible hand, a book that is much philosophical as it is historical, a rambling, digressive meditation on music, death and mythology. The manuscript begins with the following words: 'The history of the guitar is a history steeped in blood. Ever since the infant Hermes smashed a tortoise upon a rock and stretched the gut of Apollo's murdered cattle across the shell, the lyre has been the instrument of those who have entered a special contract with Death.'

On the manuscript is a note, dedicating the unfinished work to his pupil, Ivan.

As he travelled to Paris, Ivan relied upon the kindness of those he met, as he had in the years before his arrival in Vienna; but the journey was slow and he was surprised how unaccustomed he had become to the hardships of the road. From Vienna he travelled to Linz, following the line of the Danube. At Linz, he was relieved to leave the river behind as he headed for Munich, where he arrived in early November.

Whilst travelling through German-speaking lands, he survived well enough, but soon after he crossed the Rhine he found himself surrounded by speakers of French, and his luck began to give out. The weather was becoming colder. Unable to make himself understood, he was forced to sleep outside or in barns and haylofts. Paris became a kind of phantasm that hovered before him, intangible, almost mythical. He trudged through rain and biting winds, took wrong paths, found himself making ever slower progress. One night, he woke up from where he had been fitfully sleeping in the forest, and as he sat looking across the valley in the pre-dawn light, feeling a tug of homesickness as the milky sun broke through the mist, he realised that his shoes, which he had removed before sleeping, had been stolen. He set out on his way again barefoot.

By the time he reached Paris, his clothes were ripped and filthy, his flesh crawling with fleas and parasites, his body aching and sore. It seemed to him, as he trudged through the streets of the city, as if he had entered the bowels of some vast and terrible machine that turned human souls into noise—the clattering mills and factories, a roaring and bellowing that was without music. People scurried through the streets as if invisible demons pursued them, as if they had, every single one of them, received news of a dead father, mother, child or lover. Ivan's abject condition, and his inability to speak even a single word of French, meant that it took several days before he found Sor's address. He slept in backstreets or in dark corners, and made what money he could for food from playing the guitar. When he eventually arrived there, it was a Saturday. He presented the letter to a pleasant young woman—a daughter, he assumed—who spoke good German, and after a brief conversation disappeared inside, before emerging again to say that her father (ah, he thought, so he was right) was unable to take on any pupils.

Having nowhere else to go, he waited a full twenty-four hours, like an aspirant before a monastery gate, hoping that the great guitarist might take pity on him. He had no other plan, no other purpose in Paris, other than to apprentice himself to the Spaniard. So he waited through the sleet of the afternoon and the cold of the night, and he felt the gaze of the Spaniard upon him from the upper window as he sat unmoving outside the door. But when the church bells rung on the Sunday morning, he realised it was useless, that he could wait there for his entire life and would still not be admitted. He took his guitar, and he left.

He took up residence in a graveyard on a hill, watching the lights of Paris twinkle into view as the lamp-lighter did his rounds. The solitude of the road from Vienna had turned him away from a desire to consort with his fellow creatures. The dead are easy company. They demand little. Mostly, they sleep. The graveyard became his refuge and place of rest. Some tombs were lavish, sufficiently generously built to have porticoes where he could shelter from the elements: how strange, he thought, that there are those who spend money in housing the dead in such luxury and opulence, when the living go without shelter. Surrounded by the departed, feeling the weather growing colder every night, he passed the days playing the guitar in back-streets for a few coins so that he could buy food, a cough developing in his chest, the wound in his thigh that he had contracted so long ago aching every night. When he thought he was alone, with his back up against the gravestones, he played the guitar, and the music warmed him; but for much of the time, he simply sat and waited.

When Michot and Blanchard fell upon him, took him in and scrubbed him clean, dressed him in good clothes once more and told him he was to perform on the stage, Ivan—exhausted from the long journey, sick with cold and malnutrition—was already close to joining the company of the dead who were his neighbours and bedfellows, and whom he increasingly resembled. It was not out of a desire to live that he went with the two men, but out of weariness with the struggle to maintain his life. And as they helped him from the square in Montmartre where he had settled one evening to play in solitude, he knew that this was, if not his destiny, then at the very least his fate.

46

The Bulgarian guitarist's début in Paris was on the Thursday of
March the twenty-eighth, in 1827. Michot was wise enough
not to give Ivan top billing. Instead, he was squeezed towards
the bottom of the list of performers, a long way after *The Bride,
Sacrificed* **or** *The Wages of Virtue* ('performed for the third and
final time, a TRAGEDY in two acts'), after the performance of
light music by Elisabeth Campbell (violin) and Peter Mears
(Harpsichord) of London ('in which shall be included—certain
Arias by the renowned M. MOZART, adapted and arranged').
Michot had given Ivan's performance the somewhat romantic
title *Where Orpheus Once Walked*, and he had billed it as 'a
Performance of music from the High Mountain Passes of the
East,' by the guitarist Ivan Gelski, 'accompanied by Miscellaneous
Entertainments.' He was particularly pleased with 'the High
Mountain Passes of the East', for Michot understood the power
of vague mystery; he knew how, if one left a vacuum of mystery,
the imagination of the public would rush in to fill the empty
space with rumours, tales and myths so boundlessly astonishing
that no writers of cheap romances could be their equal; and he
knew that whilst the public could not be told what to approve
and disapprove—for they believed themselves, despite all evidence
to the contrary, to have minds of their own—their desires could
be moulded by the judicious use of rumour and suggestion. So
in addition to the posting of playbills, he put out a few carefully
constructed rumours about his protégé Ivan, murmuring just

the right words to this person, holding back just enough information from another, so that by the evening of the twenty-seventh of March, 1827, all of Paris seemed to be filled with whisperings about the guitarist Ivan Gelski.

On the night of the concert, whilst waiting for Misho to summon him, Ivan sat backstage looking into the dark sound-hole of the guitar. He paid little attention to the actors scurrying to and fro for their performance of *The Bride, Sacrificed.* Perhaps it was fortunate that he did not know that the melodrama being played out upon stage—a matter of mere coincidence, nothing more—concerned the abduction of a bride whilst at sea, and her eventual death in the Seraglio, her honour remaining forever undefiled. He seemed not to notice at all the shrieks and the screams coming from the stage as the actress Mademoiselle Girard was abducted, still less was he moved by her speech at the end of the second and final act when, the bride's virtue still intact, her abductor tied a stone around her neck and bade her to walk into the river, which she did whilst uttering couplets of such florid and absurd extravagance that they are quite beyond translating. Nor did the combined musical talents of Elisabeth Campbell and Peter Mears move him. Indeed, he was quite oblivious to the music, and stayed in his chair, gazing into the dark hole in the face of his guitar, remembering how as a child he had lain on the hillside and looked deep into the dark eye of the well by his mother's house.

The applause that greeted the English musicians was no less insipid than their music; and when this had died away and the hubbub of the audience—which Miss Campbell and Mr. Mears had only held in abeyance but hadn't managed to quell—began to rise again in volume, Michot stepped into the puddle of weak light provided by the theatre's gas-lamps and held up his hands. The theatre was packed, the usual rabble milling around behind the seats at the back, the foremost seats occupied by the new industrialists and merchants with their bored mistresses who toyed with their long curls. 'Now I would like to introduce you to a performance the like of which you will have never seen before,' Michot said. 'Please, I ask you to respectfully welcome Monsieur Ivan Gelski, who has travelled for many miles so that he can be here to perform tonight.'

A ripple of applause passed through the audience, and Michot scurried back-stage. A few moments later, Ivan stepped out of the wings and walked slowly across the stage, his guitar in his hand. The silence was immediate. He grasped the back of the chair that had been provided for him, and then he dragged it to the front of the stage, wood scraping on wood. He sat down and glared out at his audience. Even the rabble at the back immediately lost their taste for gossip and fooling. There, in the front row, was Ferdinand Sor, the greatest guitarist in the world, who had performed in the salons and concert halls of Paris, London and Moscow, whose mastery was unchallenged, the guitarist who had refused to take the Bulgarian as a pupil. Ferdinand had told no-one of the letter from Toepfer, or of Ivan's request. Indeed, he had come to the concert with much complaining, at the behest of Félicité, who had been excited to see this latest wonder. She was there now, by Ferdinand's side, her breasts lifting in her dress with anticipatory inhalations, her mouth slightly open, leaning forwards, her blue eyes studying the man on the stage.

He settled the guitar in his lap and closed his eyes. Then he raked his right hand over the strings, to check the tuning.

'Barbarism,' muttered Ferdinand to Félicité. 'He plays with the nails, as does Aguado.'

Félicité did not respond.

Then Ivan played a melody that started on the middle strings, played far up the fretboard where the sound was sweeter. It was the same melody he had played on that first night when he had left the settlement above Shiroka Luka, that he had first played to Toepfer; yet now he played with the refinement that came from years of study, with breathtaking glissandi and glittering sextuplets, in complex counterpoint, so that the tune echoed and re-echoed like a fugue. But the refinement he had developed in his years in Vienna seemed to intensify rather than to dilute the darkness that ran through his playing, a darkness deep and thick enough to cause a shudder in the listener. Ferdinand leaned over to Félicité. 'He has skill, of course. But the tone...'

Félicité laid her hand on Ferdinand's thigh, but did not speak.

'He plays with something of the Viennese style,' Ferdinand went on. 'He has been well trained, but the barbaric elements spoil the clarity.' Then, because Félicité was ignoring his whispered complaints, he folded his arms and sat back in his seat, an expression of displeasure on his face.

Ivan quickened his pace. The sweet purity of the melody started to take on a still darker tone. Félicité removed her hand from Ferdinand's leg, and clutched at the fabric of her dress. Ferdinand reached out to place his palm over the back of her left hand. But she did not respond, so he withdrew it again. He sighed and then shifted his body so that his back was turned slightly away from her. As he listened, he struggled to resist the music, to prevent it from taking him over, he wrestled with his heart as it strained to beat in time with those rhythms. His shoulders became hunched and a slight curl of disdain appeared at the corner of his mouth. 'What *is* this?' he muttered.

Again, Félicité did not reply.

Ferdinand looked round at the audience, and felt anger beginning to rise in him. Were the people of Paris so foolish, so shallow, that all they wanted was novelty? He reached into his pocket and drew out the handbill, and glanced through it. From the High Mountain Passes of the East... How absurd it all was. But then hadn't he been a part of the same game: the dashing Spaniard, the foreigner who made the women of London weak with his playing?

On stage, Ivan's music was building, his fingernails scything at the guitar strings with such ferocity that Ferdinand wondered whether the guitar could take it. Members of the audience were already beginning to cry out 'Bravo!' as the musician—whose head was bent low over the guitar, who showed not the slightest sign that he was even aware of the crowds before him—wove his music in ever more intricate plaits, accompanying his playing with (and here, thought Ferdinand, was the greatest barbarism of all) the occasional stamp of the foot or cry. Spectacle, Ferdinand said to himself: this is spectacle and nothing else. But everybody seemed convinced, the ignorant herd who knew nothing of art. Yet even as he was thinking these things, he knew that he was wrong and that they were right, that Félicité was right; and it stung that she was now gazing at the stage with the same look he recognised from those years in London, when as he had performed he had felt her presence and had longed for her, before they had been united, before Moscow, before they had become estranged. She was right and he was wrong. It was a hard truth, one his mind pulled back from: but there was no escaping it. This was the true music that had always eluded him. This was music that came up from the soil and the earth, from the sky and the changeable elements, born out of loves and hatreds deeper than those that he, Ferdinand, had ever dared to conceive, music that thundered in the blood as it thundered in the darkness that existed before birth and in the darkness to come after death.

Ferdinand leaned towards Félicité. 'I feel unwell,' he said.

Félicité was not listening to Ferdinand.

'I will retire early,' he said again, reaching out to take her hand.

She squeezed his hand briefly, but no more. Ferdinand got to his feet, and strode out of the concert hall, through the air that pulsed with rhythm and sound, leaving behind Ivan Gelksi's music.

Out in the street, Ferdinand stood in the light March rain, under the light of a gas-lamp. He breathed deeply of the city air that had lost every trace of the grass and the trees and the meadows, air that was purely of the city. He wished he had never heard this foreigner's music; and having heard it, he wished that he could immediately forget it. But he knew that he would not, not now and not in the future, no matter how many years might pass. He stood under the lamp-post for several minutes until he felt his heart return to normal. Then, when he heard applause raging inside the theatre—how much louder it sounded than the applause that greeted his own performances, how many more cries of 'Bravo!' there seemed—he knew it was time to leave. He could not bear to see the crowds streaming from the theatre, to hear the praises that they would heap upon the barbarian. He did not, above all, want to meet with Félicité. So he left and made his way back home through the rain and the darkness.

47

'Mademoiselle Hullin,' said Michot bowing deferentially and taking her small hand in his. 'It is wonderful you are back in Paris.' Michot had spotted the dancer from a distance off, as he stood on the staircase of the theatre looking over the crowd. He had heard that she was back in Paris, and was keen to renew their acquaintance, so he had pushed his way through the crowd to speak to her.

Félicité smiled and inclined her head in thanks. Around them swelled the excited chatter of the audience, all lingering in the hope that they might catch sight of the performer from the land of Orpheus. There was a smell in the air of human sweat, only partially veiled by the rosewater and orange blossom of the ladies' perfume. 'Monsieur Michot,' she said, 'the performance tonight...'

'Remarkable,' said Michot, smiling modestly. 'Astonishing. Monsieur Gelski is a genius of the highest order.'

'Indeed,' agreed Félicité. 'But where is he?'

Michot took Félicité by the arm. 'Come,' he said. 'Monsieur Gelski is disinclined to mingle with the public. He is an artist, you understand. And his French...'

'He speaks French?'

'Alas no, he cannot speak a single word, although he is knowledgeable in German. He studied in Venice with Karl Toepfer, a guitarist and philosopher of some talent. When we found him here in Paris, he was in the most wretched state.'

Félicité opened her lovely eyes wide.

'Blanchard and I found him in the snow, up on the hill of Montmartre. I was drawn by the sound of his music. The night was bitterly cold. I quite seriously believe that, had it not been for our timely passing, he would have died that very night.'

'Perhaps.' The tone was ironic. Félicité looked round and saw Dr. Blanchard standing by her side. He smiled at her guilelessly. 'I trust you are well?'

'Doctor Blanchard, I am so delighted.' Félicité took his hand in hers and clasped it warmly. Blanchard had attended her in sickness when she was a child, and she held the affection for him that one might have for a favoured uncle. 'My dear Doctor, it has been so many years.'

Blanchard smiled again. 'What can one do, when one's patients flee for London?' He arched an eyebrow. 'London, of all places.'

'And Berlin, and Moscow,' Félicité said.

'Indeed. But somehow you returned with a Spaniard. Most remarkable. How is your Ferdinand? I hear he is working on a new ballet.'

At the mention of the guitarist's name, Félicité looked a little pale. 'Ferdinand? My Ferdinand is in good health. But he is a serious man, Doctor.'

'He is an artist,' said Blanchard. 'Artists are always serious.'

'Oh, what you say is so true!' Félicité replied. 'But sometimes, I just want to be frivolous. And Ferdinand is so heavy with cares. There is no lightness in him, Doctor.'

Blanchard looked at her intently. 'He must love you very dearly,' he said.

'He does, Doctor. He truly does, and yet he is so very serious.'

Blanchard turned to Michot. 'It was indeed a wonderful concert.'

Michot smiled, but said nothing. The three of them were silent for a moment. 'Where is our Bulgarian friend?' asked Blanchard.

'He is backstage. He is no lover of crowds.' Michot touched the sleeve of Félicité's dress. 'Would you like to meet him?'

'Oh, yes. I would love to, Monsieur Michot. But how will I speak with him? I know no German, although my English and Russian are passably good.'

'Doctor Blanchard, I am sure, will translate.'

Blanchard sighed. 'It is late, Félicité, I am sure that Ferdinand is waiting.'

'Oh, but Monsieur Gelski seems so interesting,' said Félicité. 'Could you translate for me. For a few minutes?'

Michot smiled. 'Blanchard, please take Félicité to speak to Monsieur Gelski. I will remain here, if that does not inconvenience you.'

'Come, then,' said Blanchard. 'But he is not a man who loves conversation. You must be gentle with him.'

48

Ivan was sitting back-stage, drinking brandy, hunched over his guitar. The other performers must have already left, for there was no sign of the insipid English musicians or the cast of The Bride, Sacrificed. There was only Ivan.

When Blanchard and Félicité entered, the guitarist looked up, and Félicité thought for a moment that perhaps he had been weeping, for his eyes were rimmed with redness. Yet he did not, at first glance, seem the kind of man to weep. In this, he seemed so very unlike Ferdinand. Poor Ferdinand, who wept—it was, perhaps, the hot southern blood—at the slightest opportunity; and whilst Félicité was not without compassion, these constant tears tested her good nature. Ferdinand's tears welled up and overflowed at the most casually spoken harsh word; and when Félicité attempted to ease his sorrows with kindness, this kindness brought further tears in its wake.

But Ivan was, Félicité judged, a different kind of man. He had ungirded his waist and loosened his clothes, and he sat with his shirt half open, swigging brandy directly from the bottle. His guitar leaned against the wall to one side. He had removed his shoes, and his feet were bare. He started directly at Félicité without a trace of emotion. 'Herr Gelski,' said Blanchard quietly in German, 'I have brought Mademoiselle Hullin to speak with you. The ballerina. Perhaps you have heard of her?'

Ivan did not reply.

'Mademoiselle Hullin has performed in France, in London and in Russia. She is an extraordinary dancer.'

Again, Ivan said nothing.

Blanchard decided to try a different overture. 'The music,' he said, 'was quite wonderful.' He smiled awkwardly. 'I have never heard the like of it before.'

Ivan continued to stare with red-rimmed eyes.

'Can I ask him a question?' whispered Félicité into Blanchard's ear.

'Please, do.'

Félicité whispered again, and then Blanchard translated. 'The young lady would like to know if you are enjoying Paris.'

Ivan muttered something under his breath in Bulgarian, and then he said something in German. Blanchard moved to translate, but Félicité put her hand on his arm to still him. The rolling consonants of the guitarist's first utterance seemed both familiar and obscure to her. Félicité lightly lowered herself into a chair close to the musician and she leaned forwards so that her face was close to his. 'Doctor,' she said, 'I think we can manage in Russian.' She then spoke a few words that Blanchard could not understand. Ivan shook his head as if confused, and then said something in reply.

Félicité smiled, and said something else, a series of thick rolling consonants. Ivan rocked his head from side to side in assent. Then he put out his right hand and he clasped Félicité's own. The dancer looked down at the long nails and the rough skin. Then she smiled up at him and she spoke again. Slowly, Ivan began to reply, a word here, a word there.

Blanchard watched as the two of them exchanged stammered words in the sister languages, wrestling for common meanings and understandings. Then Ivan did something that Blanchard had not seen him do before. He smiled. It was the briefest of smiles, heavy with sadness, but it was a smile. Félicité said something that had to it the inflection of a question. Ivan looked down at their clasped hands. 'Stoyanka,' he said. 'Stoyanka.'

'Félicité,' said Blanchard, 'be careful with this man.'

The dancer looked up at her old friend. 'Doctor,' she said, 'you have no need to fear for me. Please, leave us.'

Blanchard nodded and left the dressing room, closing the door behind him. He waited outside the door, just in case.

Félicité looked at the veins lining the back of Ivan's hand, then she turned the hand over to see the broad palm. She ran the tips of her fingers along his fingernails. She murmured something else in Russian. Ivan lowered his head. Félicité reached out to stroke his hair. 'You poor man,' she murmured in French. 'You poor, poor man.'

Ivan began to weep.

49

The Wednesday after, the *Journal des Débats* published the following article.

The citizens of Paris have been blessed with the good fortune of seeing a great many talented players of the guitar, this once favoured musical instrument that, after a period of neglect, is now returning to its place of pre-eminence on the concert stage. Only last year, the great Ferdinand Sor returned from his long exile in London and Moscow. The edition of the works of the Spanish master has recently been published by M. Meissonnier, and it is a remarkable testament to his artistry and his skill.

And yet, at the moment when all lovers of the guitar in Paris believed that they could hardly be any more blessed, M. Michot from the Théâtre Montmartre presented a show with an exquisite performance by an unknown Bulgar, Monsieur Gelski. To be sure, M. Gelski cut a strange figure upon the stage; and yet his wielding of the lyre was nothing short of masterly. One can only speculate that, this musician who comes from the land of the birth of the great Thracian musician-king Orphée could have learned his art only from the direct descendants of the heroic musician of old. It was not merely the breathtaking speed of M. Gelski's ornamentation, nor the strangeness of his melodies, nor the passionate ferocity, almost the barbarism, of his rhythms: it was also the astonishing sweetness of his playing, which was after the fashion of Aguado, who uses the nails of the right hand.

We had formerly believed that M. Sor stood at the pinnacle of his art, with such a distance between him and all others who performed and composed upon the instrument, that he seemed unassailable as a god. And yet, as Ouranos once succeeded Cronos, so it seems that M. Sor has been far outstripped by this Bulgar from the Ottoman lands.

Antoine Meissonnier delivered a copy of the journal to Ferdinand in person, in the hope that he might be able to act in some way as an emollient, or that he might be able to soften the blow. He was surprised, before he even entered the apartment, to hear the sound of the piano, and he pushed open the door to find the guitarist sitting on the piano stool with manuscript paper spread across the piano top, working on some kind of composition or other. The guitarist, Antoine noted, was in a state of considerable disarray. His shirt was soiled and crumpled, and he was wearing an old house-coat with missing buttons.

When Meissonnier entered, Ferdinand hardly looked up, he just sighed. 'Antoine,' he said. 'Have you seen her?' Then he started to cough, the legacy of the long walk he had endured in the rain on the night of the concert.

Antoine hesitated, waiting for the coughing to subside. 'Who?' he asked.

Ferdinand looked round wearily, and played a dolorous chord with his left hand. 'Félicité,' he said. 'Have you seen her?'

'Today? No, not today.'

'I have not seen her since the concert with that Bulgar. I was sick that evening, Antoine. I could not stand to remain there in the concert hall.'

'It was the concert I wished to speak with you about,' said Antoine, taking a chair.

'Do you know, Antoine, Félicité has not visited me for several days.'

'I have no knowledge of Félicité's whereabouts,' Meissonnier said. 'I am here for a reason. There has been a review.'

'A review?'

'Of the concert. The Bulgar.'

'I would hope that they wrote that Monsieur Gelski was skilled, but that a skilled barbarian is still, when it comes down to it, a barbarian.' Ferdinand started to cough, his shoulders shaking.

'They wrote that he was skilled, it is true. And they spoke of barbarism. But I think you should read the rest for yourself.' Meissonier leaned over and held out the journal, but did not get up. Ferdinand pushed back the piano stool and got to his feet. He took the journal from Antoine's hand. He sat down again by the window, and his eyes skimmed through briefly.

The only sound was that of the muffled clatterings of the street outside. 'But this is monstrous,' whispered Ferdinand under his breath. 'This is absolutely monstrous.'

Antoine opened his palms. 'It is indeed. Our profits may suffer.'

'To hell with the profits. This is an affront to the Muse.'

Antoine looked past Ferdinand and out of the window. 'Ferdinand,' he said. 'I did not attend the concert. I want you to speak truthfully to me. Is what they say in the review true?'

'Of course not.' Ferdinand's denial seemed a little too emphatic. He blushed. 'No,' he said more softly, 'it is not true.'

'Then, if it is not true, there is nothing to fear,' Antoine said breezily. 'It is just one of those passing obsessions we find in the newspapers. It means nothing. Tomorrow they will have forgotten the name of Ivan Gelski, while Ferdinand Sor will be remembered for a long time to come. But if it is true, on the other hand,'—at this point, Antoine paused, and his eyes met Ferdinand's, '—if it is true, then it is no good for either of us.' He stood up and walked over to the piano, his eyes scanning the music. 'You are writing for the piano?' he asked.

'I have done so before.'

'But not for some time. Your guitar music is so popular, Ferdinand. It is so very lucrative.'

'Antoine, I do not feel like writing for guitar. Please, I do not like to display my work before it is finished.'

But Antoine Meissonnier was holding the score in his hand, scanning the staves with puzzlement. 'What is this?' he asked. 'Eleven beats to every measure?'

'Please, Antoine. Leave me in peace,' said Ferdinand.

The publisher put down the music. 'The concert next week…' he said.

'Tell them I am sick,' said Ferdinand. 'Tell them that I am sick and I will not play again.'

As Antoine left, he heard Ferdinand playing several chords on the piano in the minor key, then another bout of coughing, after which there was silence.

50

In the days that followed, Ferdinand hardly emerged from his rooms at all. He brooded by the window for hours, whilst at other times strange, disjointed piano music issued from the room. His daughter attended him dutifully, but she seemed increasingly entranced by the charms of Paris, and even whilst by her ailing father's side he sensed that she was not truly present. Often she gazed out of the window and sighed, and every time she did so, Ferdinand felt a little lonelier.

His guitar remained untouched. He had no desire to play. The strings slackened slowly and went out of tune. Antoine came to him daily, to remind him of the engagements to which he had committed himself; but Ferdinand simply told him to report he was too sick to emerge from the house. He could sense Antoine's patience growing thin. 'You are a great talent,' the publisher said repeatedly, 'You must play.'

'Yet the people want only novelty and spectacle,' Ferdinand protested. 'They would prefer a performing bear to true art.'

'Then you should return to the stage, and remind them of what true art sounds like, lest they forget.'

'But what is the point,' Ferdinand wailed, 'when the public is so dull and stupid that this Bulgar should entrance them?' Yet he could not drive the recollection of the Bulgar's performance from his mind, because in his performance there had been something that he, Ferdinand, had always aspired to but had never attained. It was not simply a difference of degree, but also a difference of kind. But what it was, this thing that he had heard in the music the Bulgar played, was something he could not define clearly, something that could not be laid hold of with the mind. The more determinedly Ferdinand pursued it, the more it slipped from his grasp, returning to nudge at the fringes of his consciousness when he was sleeping, or when he sat for long hours looking over Paris, his many exiles pressing upon him, his sense of dislocation, the knowledge that he belonged nowhere.

So Antoine continued to come, and Ferdinand continued to brood. Félicité came to see him only once. She knocked upon the door and called out, but he would not answer, and the door was locked, so she went away again, there being nothing else to do.

Meanwhile, in the theatre Ivan played several more concerts to packed audiences, and the salons began to buzz with gossip and rumour. It was said that when the Bulgar played, certain of the more impressionable women in the audience would lose consciousness and need to be revived with the use of smelling salts; and, with Ivan himself remaining taciturn and uncommunicative, incapable of conversing in French, stories and speculation proliferated. Was he a barbarian without religion, was he of the Christian faith, or was he a Moor? Was he a lover, a devourer of women, a monster, or did he live a life of celibacy like a monk? For every story and rumour there was a counter-story and a counter-rumour, and none of this did the slightest harm to Michot, who found that in a matter of days, there was the demand that he open his concert hall almost every evening. He drew up a new contract, which Ivan marked with the print of his thumb as he had before. And when, after every performance, Michot went back-stage to pay the Bulgar—for, although he was a man of commerce, he was not without fairness—he found him brooding alone with his guitar, drinking brandy. Ivan hardly glanced at the money that Michot pressed upon him. He just stuffed it into his coat without a word and turned away.

Then, one Sunday afternoon in mid-April, Antoine arrived in Ferdinand's rooms with the papers, to plead that Ferdinand should return to performing again; and what the Spaniard read was beyond his ability to bear. It was a salacious piece, published in one of the more scurrilous journals, a piece that did not charge but only hinted, and that seemed all the more persuasive thereby, because salaciousness is fed by hints and half-truths more than by blatant lies or full disclosure. In the article the two names of Félicité Hullin and Ivan Gelski were combined.

> That M. Gelski has captured the hearts of the women of Paris is well known. One only has to attend his concerts, where one can see their admiring glances, to speculate as to where these affections may end. He is a veritable Paganini of the guitar, who instils the most fervent of passions. And thus one wonders whether one could see last night, in the eyes of the exquisite dancer, Mme. Hullin, the light of an inspired affection? We cannot be sure. For it is known to the present correspondent that Mme. Hullin has enjoyed several back-stage conversations with M. Gelski, and it is to be supposed that they have many areas of mutual interest, for the Russian language, which Mme. Hullin is said to speak well, is not that far distant from the rough tongue spoken by the Bulgar...

Ferdinand recalled how he had glanced down upon the shambolic figure who had stood on his doorstep, and how he had turned him away; and he wondered if things might be different now if he had admitted him to his house. But the idea was preposterous: one cannot let every passing beggar into one's home. He tossed the paper on the floor. 'Antoine,' he said, 'have you read this?'

Antoine raised an eyebrow somewhat noncommittally.

'And is there truth in it?'

Antoine coughed. 'Doctor Blanchard has informed me that they have indeed spoken, at least once. But it is not a crime to speak to one's fellow human beings, Ferdinand.'

Ferdinand got to his feet. 'But this is insupportable,' he said. 'I will see Félicité this very evening.'

Antoine's voice was smooth. 'I am sure that there is nothing. You know how the press love rumour and insinuation.'

'I will ask her myself,' Ferdinand muttered, pulling on his coat.

51

It was already dark when Ferdinand appeared by the door of Félicité's rooms. When she heard the persistent hammering, she knew it was Ferdinand. She opened the door slowly, and for a moment he was struck again, as he had been all those years ago in London, by her luminous beauty. She was dressed simply, in a modest dress, with a shawl of fine wool wrapped around her shoulders. 'Ferdinand,' she murmured. 'You have come. Please...' She held open the door for him. She realised that, despite everything, she was pleased to see him. But there was a darkness hanging over him that made her tremble.

Ferdinand pushed past her into the room and, as Félicité closed the door, he paced up and down in agitation. Félicité seated herself on the low couch not far from the window, and watched him walking to and fro. 'What do you want, my love?' she asked.

'Your love?' The bitterness surprised her.

'Of course. You have always been my love,' she said. She pulled her shawl more closely around her shoulders, and shifted along the couch to make room for him. 'Come, let us sit for a while.'

Ferdinand stopped pacing and turned to face her. 'Félicité,' he said, 'I have loved you.'

'And I you,' she agreed. 'Now, come and sit, and we can talk.'

Ferdinand stepped towards her and then he knelt, laying his head in her lap. His shoulders began to shake, and sobs issued upwards from where he was slumped as Félicité toyed uneasily with his hair. Eventually he became quiet, and then he raised his face to Félicité and put his mouth towards hers. Félicité drew back. 'It has been so long,' she said.

'I want to lie with you,' said Ferdinand.

'Not today,' she said. 'It is my time. Later, perhaps, but not today.'

He reached up to grasp both of her arms in his hands. His eyes were unwavering. 'I want to lie with you,' he repeated. 'I will lie with you.'

'Ferdinand,' she whispered. 'Please. Not today.'

The musician did not smile. 'I will lie with you,' he said, 'whether you will it or not. It is my right.'

'No, Ferdinand.'

But Ferdinand was already tugging at her shawl, which slipped away and revealed her naked shoulders, golden in the light of the gas-lamp. He got to his feet and seated himself beside her on the couch, twisting her body with force but without roughness until her back was turned. He kissed her long beautiful neck. Félicité sighed, then stiffened and tried to pull away. But Ferdinand's hand had reached round to her breast, and the other hand was unhitching the hooks on the back of her dress. 'Please, Ferdinand,' she said, but he continued to prise apart the hooks, and peeled open her dress.

Then he stopped.

There, towards the edge of her shoulder-blade on the left hand side, were four dark crescents. Ferdinand ran his finger over them, feeling the ridges of the scars. 'And what are these?' he asked.

Félicité shrugged her shoulder and turned, so that her breast was visible. She pulled up her dress and covered herself. 'Please, Ferdinand, I have said already. It is my time, we cannot tonight.'

'The marks,' said Ferdinand. 'You have marks on your back.'

'Ferdinand,' she said, 'Please don't be like this.'

'They are fingernails, Félicité. They are the marks of a man's hand.'

'No, Ferdinand, you are mistaken. Please, stay. Let us talk. We can lie and hold each other at least. Do not be angry, my love.'

'You are marked with another man's hand.'

'No, Ferdinand, you are mistaken. There is no other man's hand. There is only you, Ferdinand.'

And who can say if what she said was true or not, for the mind when flooded with jealousy weaves strange delusions from the flimsiest of evidence; but Ferdinand was now on his feet, shaking with fury. 'You are the Bulgar's whore,' he said.

Félicité's lips opened, as if she was about to speak, but then they closed again, and she simply shook her head and closed her eyes.

She heard him leave, the slam of the door, the angry footsteps receding down the corridor; and she knew that she would not see him again.

The Barbarian

Allegro - Con Fuoco

For F. H.

Par Ferdinand Sor 1827

52

The discovery in Barcelona, in 1973, of a hitherto unpublished folio of piano works by Ferdinand, better known as Fernando, Sor created a brief stir amongst that handful of scholars who dedicate their lives to the chronicling of the history of the guitar. The manuscript had been issued by an obscure imprint in Brighton, England and was dated 1897. The front page read as follows: *Cinq Petits Pièces Elégiaques Pour Piano Forte*, Composé et Dédié à F. H. par Ferdinand Sor.

There is no other extant edition of the work, which seemingly exists only in this single copy; and the only thing on which the scholars have been able to agree is that the quality of the music is, at the very best, variable.

The first of the pieces is an unexceptional dirge in D minor called *Solitude*. This is followed by *Air: Theme and Variations*, a piece which, alas, fails to echo any of the brilliance of Sor's works for guitar. After the Air comes an Allegro, called *The Barbarian*, then a song-like piece called *Eurydice*, and finally, *Lament*.

The authorship of the work has been contested, in part because the *Cinq Petits Pièces Elégiaques* are not listed in the catalogue raisonné of Sor's works, and in part because the quality of the music is so very erratic.

The pieces have been recorded only once, in 1978, by the pianist Lance Parker. In the sleeve-notes to the recording, Parker speculates that the cycle is a musical setting of the Orpheus myth. Beginning in solitude, Parker maintains, the protagonist meets with the beautiful Eurydice, and we see the endless variations ascertained by the eye of the lover. In the third movement, Eurydice is pursued by the barbarian, the would-be rapist Aristaeus: and here the rapid passages of sextuplets, difficult to execute well, echo the sound of Eurydice's light feet on the Thracian hillside, whilst the staccato chords are the bite of the snake that is her death. The fourth movement directly takes Eurydice's name as Orpheus follows her into the underworld to save her from the grave, only to lose her with a glance. What is there left to do, Parker asks, except lament?

Parker also notes that the third movement, in its almost unprecedentedly bold use of 11/8 time, resembles the form of a Balkan kopanitsa: and yet it must be said that resemblances are only superficial. The kopanitsa is a lively dance, the beats unfolding in the pattern one-two, one-two, *one-two-three*, one-two—Quick, Quick, Slow, Quick, Quick—so that, in every bar, something is gained. In Sor's piece—if we are to accept the attribution of authorship—the beats are divided differently, one-two-three, one-two-three, *one-two*, one-two-three—Slow, Slow, Quick, Slow—so that with every bar it feels as if something is lost. This is not a piece of music that revels in something found unexpectedly, that exquisite extra beat that occasions a hop or a skip; but instead a limping, wounded time signature in which every single measure is marked by loss.

There have been no other recordings made of the work and Parker's recording has long been out of print. The *Petits Pièces Elégiaques* remain an anomaly, a possible footnote to the life of Fernando Sor, an inconvenience to be explained away. The most recent biography of the Spanish guitarist makes no mention of the work at all.

It is as if it never even existed.

53

Antoine Meissonnier looked tired. The moon was hanging low over the rooftops of Paris, and there was something melancholy in the light that it cast over the city. Ferdinand was sitting wrapped in blankets, brooding. The publisher took a sip of brandy and placed his glass down on the table. He rubbed his cheek wearily with the fingers of his right hand. Neither had said anything for the best part of an hour.

'You must return to the stage,' Meissonnier said at last. 'You cannot remain here forever in your rooms.'

Ferdinand did not say anything, did not even indicate that he had heard.

'Ferdinand,' said Meissonnier, 'this cannot continue forever. Are you to spend the rest of your days sitting here wrapped in blankets?'

Ferdinand did not reply; but it seemed, from looking at him, as if it could indeed continue forever, or at least until his death, an event that seemed strangely close to the hunched figure by the window.

'I have cancelled seven engagements already, Ferdinand. Tell me that I am not to cancel any more. The people of Paris admire you, they wish to hear you play; and yet you sit here for hour after hour, wasting your talents.'

'What do the people of Paris care?' muttered Ferdinand. 'They only care for the Bulgar. If they wish for cheap circus tricks, then they should have them. Why should I squander my talent on idiots?' It was the longest speech he had made since Antoine had arrived. The publisher took another sip of brandy.

'This Bulgar is causing nothing but trouble,' Meissonnier said quietly, looking down into his glass. 'What would you say if I proposed to take care of him?'

Ferdinand looked up, the expression on his face wretched.

'You must understand, Ferdinand, that it is not just a matter of your art. You, Ferdinand, are suffering: that I can see very well. But my profits are also suffering, and so I too am suffering.' He paused for a moment. 'There was so much promise when you came back from Russia, but now there is nothing but disarray. Look at you, sitting there swaddled in blankets like a sick man. We cannot let this continue.'

'But I am a sick man,' said Ferdinand.

'Then we must remove the cause of your sickness, so that you can be restored. If you just say the word, I will see to it that the Bulgar leaves Paris. He will be gone by Sunday.'

'How will you do this, Antoine?'

Antoine smiled thinly. 'You, Ferdinand, are an artist. That is not your concern. Just tell me if you want rid of him.'

Ferdinand settled deeper into his blankets and looked away. He sat there for a long time, without saying anything; and so, because Ferdinand did not respond, Antoine took this to be assent.

54

The following evening, when Michot came into the theatre at dusk, something seemed to be out of place. The mind is a sluggish organ: that which the body understands, the mind takes longer to grasp. So it began as a kind of creeping unease, a fluttering in the stomach, a more tentative tread than usual, a sense that the quality of light had somehow changed, or that the quality of the silence was not what it should have been, there in the empty theatre where the only presences were the ghosts of the characters—the Pierrots and Harlequins and Hamlets and Macbeths—who had passed by on the stage without leaving a trace, and the mice and the rats who scurried through the hollow walls and beneath the wooden boards. Michot walked through the quiet, empty hall, his hands flexing uneasily, the thought that there was something wrong not yet fully formed in his mind. Had anybody been there to watch his arrival, they would have said that here was a man on his guard; yet had anybody asked Michot what was wrong, he would have simply shaken himself, puzzled for a moment, before saying softly, 'Nothing, nothing at all.'

He walked down to the front of the stage, passing the empty rows of chairs to the left and right. A theatre is a sad thing when the actors and the audience have gone, when there is nothing but an empty space filled only by dust and memories. The red curtains were drawn tight shut. There was a smell in the air of mould and of damp. The gas-lamps had not yet been lit, and Michot made his way to the stage with the faint light that was filtering in through the windows as his guide.

To the right of the stage was a rope, connected to a system of pulleys so that a single tug would sweep open the heavy velvet curtains. This always seemed to Michot a melancholy moment, the opening of the curtains onto an empty stage, long before the performers and the actors had arrived.

He tugged upon the rope, hearing the creaking of fibres as they fed through the iron pulleys. It was only at this stage that he began to think, to consciously think, that there was something not right. He continued to pull. There was a sound coming from behind the curtains, like a faint thrumming of guitar strings.

When he curtains were open, what he saw at first made no sense to him. It was as if a shadow had taken on form above the stage, as if a hole had been cut in the world. Something dark hung from the ceiling, a shape that did not resolve into anything clear or certain. Michot climbed the steps onto the stage and looked up. He could hear the sound again, clearer now that the curtains had been pulled wide. He moved a fraction, the light changed, and he saw what it was.

Ivan Gelski was suspended from the ceiling, his hands lifted high above his head, his face blackened with drying blood, a smashed guitar suspended around his neck. His bare and bruised feet were several yards above Michot's head, pointing downwards to the boards below. It seemed for a few moments as if he was floating there without anything suspending him, but when Michot looked closer, he saw the thin filaments of guitar strings wrapped around the guitarist's wrists. The strings had been tied to a rope, and this in turn had been slung over the roof beam. The man was not even twitching.

Michot stood for a few moments, looking up at Ivan's body as it gently twisted to and fro, a few degrees clockwise, a few degrees anticlockwise. It took several seconds more for his mind to catch up. It was only then that he heard the man's voice, no more than a whisper, coming as if from an enormous distance, up there in the gloom above the stage: 'Misho!'

Michot staggered down the steps that led from the stage. At the bottom of the steps, he paused for breath, his hand reaching out to the stage to steady himself. He breathed deeply, twice, then swore. Without looking back, he ran down the aisle, out into the fading light of the evening.

55

In the street Michot shouted for help, waving his hands in an attempt to enlist the assistance of passers-by. Several stout citizens came to his assistance, evidence that there is still some goodness in the world. He returned into the dark of the theatre accompanied by three men. They climbed onto the stage and all four of them looked up at the figure that hung above them, unmoving. Michot took one of the men and hurried backstage to collect a ladder for the deposition. The other two men stood, looking anxiously upwards as the figure swayed in the rapidly failing light.

Michot and his assistant returned with a ladder. They propped it against the roof-beam and Michot climbed to the top—he had a good head for heights. The next part of the operation was delicate. The other men dragged a table from behind-stage and placed it under the hanging man's feet, then two of them climbed upon the table and reached up so that they could just about touch the feet of the hanging man: they were still warm. There was a stench of human shit.

Michot busied himself with the knot. When it came loose, the body slipped several feet, almost unbalancing Michot from the beam where he was perched. The men standing on the table took up the strain, taking the weight of the body, and the rope went taut again. In this way they guided him down onto the table, where they laid him horizontal, like a corpse.

Michot climbed down from the beam whilst the other men

were lifting the broken guitar from around the musician's neck. The face of the guitar had been smashed, and the strings removed so that they could be turned into the tools for the guitarist's torture. The darkness in the theatre was thickening, and Michot could not clearly make out the extent of the damage that had been done. The strings, twisted filaments still attached to the wrists, glinted in the scarce light. The man had been beaten around the face and his cheek and lip were split. He let out a faint groan, and his eyelids flickered, but he did not move. Michot turned to one of his associates. 'Tell me,' he said, 'do you know Doctor Blanchard?'

'I do, yes.'

'Then may I ask you to fetch him, to tend to this man's wounds?'

'Of course.'

He left the theatre at a run, leaving Michot and the two others keeping vigil over the body. The chest still rose and fell a little, but the eyes remained closed. The light in the theatre continued to fade. Michot sat down on stage, on a log that the night before had been used in a dramatic performance to seat a sea-nymph, and he listened to the uneven breath of the man who lay on the table. The other men climbed down from the stage, where the stench was horrible, and sat down in seats in the front row, looking about themselves fretfully. It seemed an age before Blanchard appeared in the doorway, coming at a run with his bag under his arm. Michot rose to his feet and hurried from the stage, meeting his friend in the aisle. They conferred for a few moments in low voices, then Blanchard strode up to the stage where the man lay on the table.

The doctor put his bag down and leaned over the table. 'There is not enough light,' he said. 'Michot, fetch a gas-lamp so I can work. And brandy.'

Michot went to the dressing room back-stage and fetched

Ivan's brandy and a lamp. He lit the lamp, and returned to the stage carrying the light, and passed the brandy to Blanchard. 'Hold it,' said Blanchard. 'Hold it so I can see.' Michot lifted the lamp so that it threw yellow light over the body. He turned his face away.

The guitar strings had cut deep into the flesh of the wrists. The left hand was worse than the right with two silver-wound strings and one of gut disappearing into a dark rent in the swollen flesh. The strings on the right hand cut less deeply, but there was still an open wound that ran from the inside centre of the wrist all the way round to the back of the hand. Several fingers on each hand were broken. In the light, it was now evident that the victim had soiled himself as he had hung there. His shoes had been removed, and the soles of the feet were badly bruised, as if they had been beaten with clubs or cudgels. Blanchard took a deep breath and opened the bottle of brandy. He moved to the head of the body, prised open the mouth, and poured in a large dose. The man let out a faint growl, a thin rivulet of brandy ran from his mouth, and then he swallowed. The three men who had come to assist from the street waited in the front row, for having unexpectedly arrived in the theatre in the middle of this drama, it was as if they had no other choice than to stay to the end.

Blanchard set about checking for further injuries. He went about his business methodically, as if he was oblivious to the smell and the horror. Michot kept his own face averted. At last Blanchard straightened up. 'Some ribs on the left-hand side are broken,' he said, 'and the fingers too. It looks as if they were broken before he was hanged. There may be a fracture in his arm as well. It is hard to tell. The feet are damaged, but not irreparably so. But these wrists...' Blanchard shook his head. He reached into his bag and took out some small scissors. He spent the next few minutes skilfully snipping through the wire.

He did so with the utmost delicacy, but it was necessary more than once for him to prise open the wounds on the wrists, and to insert the scissors into the flesh so that he could cut the tangled strings free. When he did so, the victim turned fitfully on the table. Blanchard carefully placed the strings to one side, and then he doused the wounds in brandy. 'No morphine,' he muttered, almost to himself, wiping his hands on a cloth. Then he turned to his old friend. 'Monsieur Michot,' he said acidly, 'this man was in your care.'

'Blanchard,' Michot snapped, 'without my intervention, he would already have been dead. You saw the state he was in when we found him sitting in the snow that night in Montmartre.'

Blanchard rubbed his forehead. 'We must get him to the hospital. Tell me, who could have done this thing?'

Michot did not reply.

'Well,' said Blanchard, 'this, at least, is certain: they have done a good job. Monsieur Gelski will not play again.'

56

They flagged down a coach. Michot and Blanchard sat on either side of the wounded man, who did not open his eyes, but merely groaned every few moments. The broken guitar rested on Michot's lap. As they arrived at the hospital, it started to hail. Blanchard paid the coachman, and they half dragged and half carried Ivan into the building. The physician on duty, an old friend of Blanchard's, raised his eyebrows but said nothing. 'The man is sick,' Blanchard said. 'His wounds need dressing. He needs morphine. Please, is there a bed for him?'

With the help of some assistants, they conveyed the musician to a suitable place in a gloomy ward where pale ghosts coughed and shivered and groaned in their beds. Somebody ran to bring a gas-lamp. Blanchard stowed the guitar underneath the bed-frame.

'Leave us,' he said, turning to Michot. 'Go back to the theatre. There will be people arriving soon. There's nothing more you can do here.'

Michot looked relieved. He nodded in assent and disappeared into the corridor and then out into the street, where the hail was coming down with increasing ferocity. He called another coach and made his way back to the theatre.

Blanchard called for hot water, morphine and clean cotton cloths. He administered a few drops of morphine, to keep the patient quiet, then he removed the soiled clothing. Once the man was naked before him, he started to swab away the dried blood from the man's face and beard, and then moved on to wash the rest of the body. The wounds to the face were not severe, and required little in the way of dressing. He turned his attention to the hands, where matters were more serious. He carefully wiped away the blood. The patient had lost significant amounts of blood, but not so much that his life was in danger. Blanchard took some bandages, and started to wrap the hands and the wrists, to protect the wounds. Next he turned his attention to the feet, binding them with bandages. The ribs would be able to look after themselves, he judged, as long as the patient did not move too far or too suddenly. When he was done, he administered another couple of drops of morphine. He straightened up, went to the basin where he washed the blood from his hands, then rubbed his back. He took his watch out of his pocket and glanced at it. It was almost nine. Outside it was dark, and the hail had turned to bitterly cold rain. 'Look after this man,' he said to the doctor on duty. 'He does not speak French, only German. When he comes round, call for me. I want to speak with him.'

The duty doctor raised an eyebrow. 'These injuries,' he said, 'they are unusual.'

'Hung by his guitar strings.'

The other doctor frowned, but said nothing.

'When he wakes up, call for me,' said Blanchard. 'I want to find out who did this. I want to bring whoever it was to justice. One would have thought that in this damned country we would, by now, have suffered enough of bloodshed and of barbarity.'

Doctor Blanchard left the hospital to face the implacable anonymity of the rain.

57

Some time in the middle of the night, as the rain continued to fall in the streets, Ivan opened his eyes and gazed at the ceiling from where he lay on his hospital bed. His head and body were heavy with the pain and the morphine, but the morphine could not drive out the clarity of his remembering.

He had not recognised the men who came to take him the day before. They had faces of studied anonymity, the kind of faces that depart from the memory the moment they have been encountered. There were seven of them, all of them strong. They came to his lodgings in the early afternoon, and took him by the arms. One man went inside and collected Ivan's guitar. Then the men led the Bulgar to the Grand Théâtre de Montmartre. Ivan walked with them. He did not struggle or protest. Nor did he say a single word. He walked with his head down.

When they arrived at the theatre, one of the men unlocked the door—who knows where he found a key? And once inside, they hauled Ivan towards the stage. One of them pulled open the curtains. After the curtains had creaked open, they pushed Ivan up the steps. It was only then—once they were on the stage where so many are beaten and killed and tormented night after night, but wholly without consequence—that they began to jeer and curse him in words he did not understand. Four of the men took up heavy clubs and started to beat him. Ivan fell to the floor. As his body shrank away from one blow, they countered it with another. There was nowhere he could go, nowhere except deeper into the pain and humiliation and suffering, no exit from the horror, no respite. The three remaining men smashed the face of his guitar and unwound the strings from the pegs. Then, the ones with the cudgels put them down on the floor and pinned Ivan to the stage. One of the others broke his fingers, each one in turn, the crack made by each surprisingly loud in the empty auditorium. One this was done, another two took his wrists and tied the guitar strings around them. They bound the strings to a rope with careful knots. Somebody fetched a ladder and climbed it, threading the rope over the roof-beam. Another looped some rope around Ivan's neck and tied the guitar to him. Then they hauled the victim up towards the rafters, and they tied off the rope. As Ivan ascended, he let out a bellow of pain, and he continued bellowing until he was as high as he could go. Then Ivan was silent.

The men who had done all this had nothing against their victim. They did not know the name Ivan Gelski. They did not even know who had ordered this torment. All they knew was that they had families to feed, and that when they left the theatre, they would find someone waiting for them who would thrust money into their hands, so that by the time the sun was sinking low in the sky they would be at home with their children clambering upon their knees, and would take the money from their breast-pockets to show to their wives, and they would be rewarded with smiles and caresses, because hunger was kept at bay for another few days. Having seen that the job was well done, they closed the curtains, and left the theatre by the same way that they had come.

Ivan hung in the darkness, the guitar strings by which he was suspended thrumming occasionally as his body twisted to and fro. And if the Virgin Mary Eleusa, to whom he had been entrusted so many years before, had looked down that afternoon at this broken man, perhaps even she would have been surprised by what she saw. For in the agonising moments of that terrible ascent, as the strings of the guitar tugged and cut at the flesh of his hands and his wrists, something in Ivan changed. The bitterness born the day Stoyanka was taken from him, the fury he had tended each winter in Skopje and loosed upon the hillsides of the Rhodopes every summer, the anger that only the music of the Jew, Solomon, had been able to soothe, the darkness that he had resisted through the long years in Vienna by playing of melodies upon his guitar, the cool sweetness of the music that was the only thing capable of quenching his boiling hatred—at that moment, as the hired thugs hauled him to the ceiling, as the strings sliced his flesh, something miraculous took place, and he was pierced by a kind of gentleness that seemed to slice deep into him, cutting away as it did so every trace of bitterness. The pain of his torment was dreadful and vast; and yet, in that moment of agony, as the pain spread to encompass the entire world, the men who had tortured him hurrying down the aisle and out into the daylight, having drawn the curtains on that terrible scene, at the moment when it seemed as if there was nothing other than pain and darkness and infinite aloneness, in his soul was born a sweet melody like the sound of a distant lyre plucked on a hillside generations before; and as he closed his suffering eyes, his body relaxed as if for the first time, settling into the pain and the joy of the world, and he knew then that now, at last, this music, this peace, would never leave him.

58

When a messenger came from the hospital the following morning, it was not with the news that Blanchard had hoped. It had been a wretched night, the rain turning to snow and the snow, in the early hours, to an ugly sleet that covered everything in the city with a freezing brown sludge. The messenger's shoes were soaked through, and he panted for breath. 'Dr. Blanchard,' he gasped, 'you must come to the hospital quickly.'

'Is there a problem?' asked Blanchard.

'The patient is gone.'

'He is dead?' Doctors, those priests of life and of death, have no use for euphemisms.

'No, he is gone.'

'How can he be gone? He was dosed with morphine. His feet were damaged. He had no shoes. And this weather...'

'But he is gone. His bed is empty. Come and see.'

Blanchard struggled into his coat and left his apartment. They made their way through the icy streets to the hospital. When they arrived, another doctor was on duty. Blanchard nodded but said nothing. The doctor led him to the empty bed.

Blanchard pulled back the blanket. The sheet was marked with blood that could trace, if one used sufficient imagination, the broken body of the man who had lain there, a hovering image of a wounded man. How easy it would be to pin upon these few marks elaborate dreams of other worlds, tales of miracles and of wonders and of divine providence. But Blanchard was not a man inclined towards such dreams. For him, it was only cotton and blood and the impression of a man's body, a fathom long. Blanchard stooped to look underneath the bed. The guitar was gone too.

Doctor Blanchard stared for a while at the marks that were the only remaining signs of Ivan Gelski, then he pulled the blankets back into place and sat down on the edge of the bed where he gazed out of the window at the grey clouds that were slowly rolling across the sky.

59

It did not take long for the newspapers to forget about Ivan. The story of his torment and disappearance caused something of a sensation, even though it only reached the ears of the public in breathless and confused form, with all the melodrama, half-truth and speculation one might expect. The press continued to speculate for a few days, but rumour, alas, needs something to work on—a hint or a suggestion or at the very least another rumour—and when it became clear that Ivan was not returning, and that there was nothing more to be said about the case, the newspapers soon started to lose interest. Whether he had taken that final journey from which, the sages solemnly tell us, nobody can possibly return (in which case, one of the more lyrical correspondents maintained, he would have had no use of a guitar, for he would, all being well, have had a celestial harp awaiting him), or whether he had simply fled the city (which would have been all but impossible, others insisted, given the wretchedness of the weather that night and the condition of the man), it was clear that he was gone, and that he would not be returning. Within a matter of days, it began to seem as if Ivan had hardly existed at all, only as a dream conjured by the bored citizens of Paris, a diversion that was quickly gone.

After Ivan's disappearance, Michot's theatre started to go into decline. By 1830, in the face of plunging takings and increased costs, Michot declared himself bankrupt. He fled his debts, first to London, where he shivered miserably in the mist for a few months before taking a ship to the New World. He spent his final days, more or less happily, in the Caribbean. Blanchard retired early in 1832—he had some independent means, and few desires to be fulfilled. He left Paris for a villa in a small village outside Lyons, and thenceforth dedicated himself to his theoretical studies. Sometimes, as he sat on his veranda looking out over the valley, he thought of the sufferings of Ivan Gelski, and of the man's disappearance, and the thought filled him with melancholy that could not be dispelled even by an entire bottle of the excellent local wine. Fernando Sor emerged from isolation towards the end of 1827. His ballet, *Le Sicilien*, was performed in the June of that year and was a critical failure. He did not recover his position until the following year when he returned to the concert stage, and again found himself extolled as the greatest of the exponents of the guitar. By this time, he had severed his links with Antoine Meissonnier in favour of another publisher, Pacini; but despite the accolades bestowed upon him until his death, Sor spent the remainder of his days increasingly swathed in self-doubt, gloominess and solitude.

It was not long after the Bulgar disappeared, that the dancer Félicité Hullin left Paris also. She made directly for Moscow, where she returned for a while to the stage and then settled as a ballet teacher. She sent no replies to the letters that Ferdinand mailed her every autumn. She was married a decade later, to a teacher of the French language who was ten years her senior. At the precise time of her marriage, Ferdinand, grieving the death of his daughter due to sickness, himself fell ill.

Then, one morning in Moscow, as Félicité's unborn child lay coiled in her womb, the newly-married dancer awoke and gazed over the river Moskva as it glittered in the early morning sun, and she thought with a trace of sadness of Ferdinand, whose previous letter had seemed so filled with sadness and regret. It was early summer, in the year of 1839. Somewhere in Paris,

Ferdinand was taking his last breaths, in the company of two Spanish friends, an exile to the last.

He was buried in the Cimetière Montmartre. That autumn, Félicité received no letter from Paris.

Part Four

The Saint

60

Some time in the late afternoon, the woodcutter Boyko lay down in the shade of an old rowan tree and looked up to the sky above. It was a hard living, the days spent in the forest cutting wood. His back was bent from carrying logs and kindling. He had lost a finger to an infection brought on by a splinter. He had removed the finger himself, with the axe he used for chopping wood. But it was bitterness that had caused his spine to bend and his brow to furrow. He lived without wife or family, he drank from the stream and ate what the hillsides provided. The little money he earned from selling wood he used to buy bread, cheese, and the rakiya that enabled him to go on living.

The flies buzzed around his head and the sun slanted over the hillside. It was only when the night chill started to come in that Boyko got to his feet and loaded the logs upon his back, making sure that they were well secured. He would be home before dark. He started to trudge across the hillside towards the pine wood. It was then that the stranger stepped from the shadows.

He was large and roughly dressed, and a beard covered his face. In the fading light Boyko saw pale bandages on the man's hands. Then he looked at the stranger's face, and Boyko recognised him instantly. 'Ivan,' he said, his voice wavering with the sudden tears. 'You have returned.' Slung on Ivan's back, Boyko saw the instrument that had once belonged to Solomon, and his first thought was this: Ivan has come, at last, to seek revenge.

But on seeing the guitar, Boyko also felt ashamed. He was ashamed of the way that they had killed Solomon, nailed to a cross that was lifted high on the hillside above Shiroka Luka, ashamed of the blood he had shed, of the manifold cruelties of his days in the mountains. Since the day Ivan had left, when Boyko had let his gun fall into the stream, he had not killed again; but now Ivan was returned, and Boyko trembled with shame and fear. He wanted to turn his away his gaze, but could not.

'Boyko,' said Ivan softly, 'put down your load.'

Boyko hesitated, so Ivan repeated his command. But it was only when he commanded him for a third time that Boyko shrugged off the burden of logs and kindling. He straightened up and looked into Ivan's eyes. 'You have come for revenge,' he said.

Ivan stepped forward several paces, and reached out a bandaged hand. He touched Boyko on the arm. And at this moment, Boyko heard music, a sound like that of plucked strings. Then Boyko, who had always had about him something of the grimness of a priest, and for whom music was an impenetrable mystery, felt tears in his eyes. The bitterness he had imagined was there forever began to bleed out of him; and in its place there was a kind of peace, as if a softly breathing bird had come to roost in his soul, tipped back its head and begun to sing with a music of such sweetness that no amount of torment could drown it out entirely. Boyko closed his eyes. His body relaxed as if for the first time, and he settled into the world's misery and into the world's joy. He felt Ivan's arms embrace him. 'Ah, Boyko,' Ivan whispered, 'friend Boyko.'

Ivan released him, and Boyko opened his eyes. The music dispersed into the flutter of evening birdsong. Ivan did not smile. 'It is good to see you Boyko. May God be with you.' Then Ivan raised a bandaged hand, as if in blessing, and turned away into the forest. Boyko stood there for a long time in silence. The evening star blazed in the heavens. When the moon started to rise, he gathered his logs and made his way home.

61

For a while, the stories spread from hillside to hillside and from village to village: tales of Ivan, the saint with the bandaged hands. First, the tale told by the woodcutter Boyko, then, a year later, a man with the pox who was touched by the bandaged hand of a stranger, heard music, and was cured. After that, the broken-hearted lover, lamenting by the stream where the wagtails cocked their heads, who encountered a strange, gentle figure who touched him with bound hands, and filled him with a music that left no more room for grief. The tales spread, a plague of murmurings and rumours. And who can say which of these stories were true? Who can untangle the knotted yarns that run throughout the world? The best we can do is this: to take up these fibres and work them into threads, and weave these threads into blankets that might keep at bay the cold of the night. It is better, after all, than twisting them into ropes, in order that we might hang ourselves or each other.

The stories multiplied for a while; but then, after five years, perhaps six, this stream of stories began to dry up; and one day in the late autumn, an old shepherd was making his way home past the place called Trigrad, by the Devil's Throat where the stream plunges into the earth through the wide crevice between the rocks, and where legend says that Orfei entered the underworld in pursuit of his true love. But this shepherd was not thinking of Orfei, or of love, or of streams of stories; he was thinking only of the path home, and of the tiredness he carried with him. And as he passed the moss-covered rocks, where rainbows hovered in the spray, something caught his eye: a shattered instrument, like a tambura or a lyre, lying amongst the green ferns just to one side of the opening that led into the depths of the earth.

The shepherd clambered onto the rocks and reached out for the instrument. He picked it up, turning it over in his hands, examining closely its broken face, scraping at the grease that still clung to the frets. The strings were long gone.

He was no musician, this shepherd. All the music he needed was the sound of the hills and streams and the lamenting of sheep. But he carried the instrument home nevertheless, and showed it to his wife. She did not know what to say, and he had no use for it, so he placed it in the corner, and forgot about it until the winter was well advanced.

Sometime the following year, in the depths of February, a particularly cold wind came howling up the gorge to Trigrad. Snow lay heavily upon the hills, and even when piled with sheepskins and blankets, the people shivered in their houses at night. The rivers and streams stood still, and in the pond that lay not far from the village, a duck could be seen, as if suspended in tumbling flight, trapped in the ice. The shepherd woke one morning after a night of shivering and, too weary to cut logs for kindling, took the guitar and broke it into pieces. He broke up the fragments of wood, piled them together in the hearth and lit them. Soon a small fire was driving out the cold from his mountain house. His wife came and squatted by his side, her hands towards the flames. The fire lasted only a short while; but its memory sustained them for another two or three days, until the thaw at last began. For the body, and not only the soul, also cries out to be warmed.

62

Memory, however, persists; and even today, if you travel in those parts, you might find an old person willing to stop and talk, one who has no liking for the hubbub of the city, who will sit with you on the stone step of their house in the evening and feed you with white cheese, who will ply you with plum brandy made with the fruit that still grow on the hillside, and who will point to the constellations and reminisce about the past, complaining about city folk and their restless ways.

You too are one of these restless city folk; but perhaps you both pretend, for a while, that you are somehow different; and so, half-drunk, seduced by soft laughter and the insect orchestra of the hillsides, making your way through the language as one might stumble across an unfamiliar landscape in the dead of the night, you might begin to piece together the tales of Saint Ivan, who cured by means of his music; and you might hear, or imagine you hear—it really is so hard to tell—how your host's five times great-grandfather encountered the saint on the hillside, and how he, too, was cured. And as you lie in your hotel bed, you might dismiss these as the tales of old folks, half addled by the passage of the years and by plum brandy.

But then, the next morning, you head up the hillside and, after following the path a little while, you come across a small whitewashed chapel. Finding the door unlocked, you go inside. Christ gazes down from the domed ceiling, and the four Evangelists look on from the niches around the dome: but it is the image on the far wall that takes your attention: a saint, with dark beard and eyes turned to the heavens, his bandaged hands raised in prayer and, in his lap, the shape of a guitar.

The sweat from the climb is cooling on your body. Unbeliever that you are, you lean forwards and lay a flower that you have picked in the meadow on the ledge before the image. Then—because it seems the right thing to do, because there is nobody else here to witness your act, because the saint is staring down at you with undiminished gravity—you go down on your knees, close your eyes, and you listen.

It is then, as you kneel there in the chapel, that you hear it for the first time: from the sigh of the wind in the trees and the heart's fragile beating, from the incessant buzz of the insects and the call of the birds, coalesces the sweetest music, as if Orpheus himself were passing with his lyre, as if, for a moment, you are offered a glimpse of a time before all of this hubbub and uproar, before you or even the saints were born, when the world was young and the forests were filled with bears and with wolves.

Some say it is Saint Ivan of Gela, playing his music to all the angels of heaven; others that it is simply the sound of the world running its course.

ACKNOWLEDGEMENTS

This book was a long time in the making, and would not have been possible without the help of a great many people and organisations. In researching the book, I made three trips to Bulgaria. The third and longest of these trips, in 2007, was funded by Arts Council England.

One of the reasons I kept on coming back to Bulgaria was that I was extraordinarily well looked-after. In Sofia, Hristina Vucheva helped me make some inroads into the mysteries of the Bulgarian language, whilst in Plovdiv, Mariyana Georgieva and family were wonderful hosts, and took me to places I never would have found unaided. Yassen Dimitrov not only opened his home to me, but also was a good sounding-board for the story I was writing. Many others generously gave of their time and hospitality in Bulgaria. I am grateful in particular to Mary Zell in Belitsa, Georgi Ivanov in Devin and Emily Hallar in Sandanski.

My third research trip was overland from the UK by train, and so I should also thank Frank and Tia O'Connor in Bucharest, and in Paris, Benjamin Saragalia, Charlotte Opoires, and Laurence Pascal. Elee Kirk shared the first part of this particular journey with me, as well as providing constant encouragement throughout the gestation of this book, whilst Peter Gear shared the homeward leg: I am grateful to both of them for their companionship on the road. Thanks are also due to Bob Kerr, who first taught me the classical guitar, and has thus provided me with a lifetime's pleasure.

Back in the UK, several other people helped out with archival and historical research. In particular, James Westbrook in Brighton was extremely generous in sharing his knowledge of the classical guitar in the nineteenth century, and giving me access to an extraordinarily rich archive of unpublished material. *The Descent of the Lyre* is, of course, a work of fiction, but during the research there have been a few published works to which I have repeatedly returned. I am indebted for detailed background on Fernando Sor's life to Brian Jeffrey's superb biography, *Fernando Sor: Composer and Guitarist,* published by TECLA; and for an insight into Bulgaria's long and fascinating history, Thomas Butler's *Monumenta Bulgarica*, published by Michigan Slavic Publications, has been invaluable. I also do not know what I would have done without Mercia MacDermott's *Bulgarian Folk Customs*, published by Jessica Kingsley, a book extraordinarily rich in insights into Bulgarian folklore and traditional belief.

In addition, throughout the writing of this book, I have been supported by a great number of friends and colleagues. I should thank, in particular, my agent Marilyn Malin, and at De Montfort University, Simon Perril, Kathy Bell and Jonathan Taylor. Finally, the idea for this book was planted in my head some fifteen years ago when Sue Shone asked me to write her a story about a guitarist's hands. I remain grateful for this initial impetus: Sue—it was a long time coming, but I got there in the end.

ABOUT THE AUTHOR

Will Buckingham writes both fiction and philosophy. His books include *Goat Music* (2015, ROMAN Books), *Cargo Fever* (2007, Tindal Street Press) and *Finding Our Sea-Legs* (2009, Kingston University Press). He is Reader in Writing and Creativity at De Montfort University.